God's Hazard

Library of Congress Cataloging-in-Publication Data

Mosley, Nicholas, 1923-
 God's hazard : a novel / by Nicholas Mosley. -- 1st ed.
    p. cm.
 ISBN 978-1-56478-540-4 (pbk. : alk. paper)
 1. Father and child--Fiction. 2. God--Fiction. I. Title.
 PR6063.O82G63 2009
 823'.914--dc22

                          2008046264

Funded in part by a grant from the Illinois Arts Council, a state agency,
and the University of Illinois at Urbana-Champaign

www.dalkeyarchive.com

Cover: design by Danielle Dutton, illustration by Nicholas Motte
Printed on permanent/durable acid-free paper and bound
in the United States of America

GOD'S HAZARD

a novel
by Nicholas Mosley

Dalkey Archive Press
Champaign and London

PART ONE

1

An Old Man walks in his Garden. He is trying to think of a way to get his now grown-up children to leave home. He does not want to turn them out, because then they would resent him. He wants to remain on good terms with them when they are out of the Garden, because he hopes still to be able to help them. On the other hand, they should be learning to be free of him.

A knotty one, this. The Old Man sits with his back against a tree. A knot is where a branch might grow out horizontally from a tree. A knot is what one finds oneself tied up in when one tries too hard to be rational.

There is such stillness in the Garden! Everything rushes outwards and comes together all at once. Light stands still.

The Old Man's wife, Lilith, comes into the Garden. She says 'You look as if you're waiting for something to fall on your head from that tree.'

He says 'I'm trying to think of a way to get the children to leave the Garden.'

'Why not just tell them to go?'

'Because that would seem uncaring.'

'But you want them to be free of you.'

'Yes, but I want them to know I still care for them.'

She says 'And for them still to care about you!'

He thinks – She is trying to tie me in knots? He says 'Anyway, as things are, I think they're getting a bit fed up.'

Lilith sits beside him with her back against the tree. She faces at right angles to the way in which the Old Man is facing. She thinks – A branch might grow horizontally from the tree and stretch over the edge of the Garden.

She says 'You want it all ways up and down and sideways all at once.'

He says 'Yes, that's what I do.'

'Why not just tell them there's something they can't do? Then when they do it, it would be reasonable to get them to leave the Garden.'

'Being reasonable isn't caring.'

'No, but they'd have to learn that.'

'Anyway, what if they don't do what I tell them not to?'

'Then they wouldn't be grown up, would they?'

The Old Man considers this. He wonders – Is she being reasonable, difficult, or clever?

He says 'All right, but I've told them that they're no longer children. That grown-ups are responsible for themselves.'

'So –'

'So is it or is it not being responsible if they choose not to be?'

Lilith thinks about this. She says 'You're tying yourself in knots.'

'Yes, so that they can be free.'

She thinks – And then you will become free?

Then – But you can't do becoming, you do being –

– So is that where I come in?

She says 'Perhaps I can help you.'

'How?'

Lilith leans over on one elbow and looks over the edge of the Garden to where there are figures working in the fields far below. She thinks – Perhaps I can get one of the workers to come in on this.

The Old Man says 'I mean, I don't want them to think I'm a shit.'

She says 'But grown-up people will probably love shits.'

'You think so?'

'All part of the life-force, evolution, and so on.'

She thinks – I might get that attractive chap with a scythe to tell them they can do something they're supposed not to do.

The Old Man says 'But it won't do them any good if they think I'm a shit.'

'Well they'll have to work that one out for themselves, won't they?'

The Old Man thinks about this. He says 'We'll all get in a terrible muddle.'

She says 'It's language that gets in a muddle. You shouldn't have given them language if you don't want them to get into knots.'

'I wanted them to be different from animals.'

'Well you can always help them to get unknotted when the time comes.'

The Old Man thinks some more about this. It is as if he is still hoping for something to fall on his head from the tree. He says 'But when they're grown up they should think they're doing it all themselves.'

She says 'But that's where I come in.'

'They don't even know that you exist!'

'Exactly.'

'What?'

'They'd think they were doing it themselves.'

The Old Man stops thinking. A light seems to come on his head. He says 'That's brilliant!'

Lilith says 'Hasn't anyone told you you've got a brilliant wife?'

2

A man who had been christened Adam sat in front of his laptop computer. He thought – But I am not fitted for this. His fingers tangled on the keys as if following a jangling in his head. He thought – The electronics in my brain transmit themselves to the electronics in the computer. As if in response to this the text on the screen now became jammed. Adam pressed various buttons and nothing happened. He pressed 'Save,' and nothing that he could see happened. He wondered – Does God sometimes press 'Save' and nothing happens?

– We all get tied up in knots?

His wife Evie came into the room. She said 'I've brought you the papers.'

He said 'What's been happening?'

'There's some sort of bomb scare at Sophie's school.'

'Let me see.'

'It's not in the papers. I've been telephoned by one of the mothers.'

Adam took the papers. The headlines were about wars in the Middle East; about how world leaders were insisting that the best chance of peace was to let war go on a bit longer.

She said 'Are you listening?'

He said 'What did the mother say?'

'She didn't know. It's just that there are police outside the school and they're not letting anyone through.'

He thought – Some sort of hostage-taking?

He said 'It might be one of their tricks.'

'What tricks?'

'They're an odd lot at that school. They've got a new science mistress who gets them to do experiments.'

'Experiments with life?'

'Well that's science, isn't it?'

Adam unplugged his computer and turned it over on his lap. He prised the battery out of its slot, waited a few seconds, then put the battery and the plug from the mains back in. He thought – It's like changing a nappy. Or you might sometimes have to wipe out the whole bloody thing and start again.

He said 'Wasn't there some plan for them to go on an expedition today?'

'That science mistress, she sounds crazy.'

'They love her.'

'Have you finished?'

'I'm just worried that I mightn't have pressed "Save."'

He pressed the Start button and waited while bits of light flickered, then shapes like beetles moved in a slot across the screen. He manoeuvred an arrow to where it said 'Enter your name,' then to a logo that represented the text on which he had been working. He waited until his text came up and then pressed 'Save' again. He said 'Yes, that should do the trick.'

He wondered – Are humans given a second chance to be saved?

Evie said 'What are you writing now?'

'A reinterpretation of the Book of Genesis.'

'Oh is that all!'

He clicked 'Start' again and then 'Turn Off Computer.' He thought – In my beginning is my end; or is it the other way round?

He said 'All right I'm coming.'

'You think we should go to the school?'

'What else can we do?'

He found himself wishing he had taken more trouble to remember his last sentence so that he could go on with the story in his mind. Was it about Lilith being a brilliant wife?

Going down the stairs from the attic room where he worked, Adam was thinking – But I often can't remember even what I am trying to do. What for God's sake is God's hazard? – A hazard is a complex manoeuvre with the chance of things going wrong? – Humans can't have freedom without the risk of things going wrong? God himself must have wanted something a bit more lively? – And I mean, this is a story. A story is the best way to describe things which can be described in no better way.

In the street there did not seem to be much happening. Adam went ahead with Evie trailing slightly behind him. She said 'What are you saying about Genesis?'

'I'm saying we've given God a frightfully bad press. I'm standing up for him.'

'Who's given him a bad press?'

'The people who wrote Genesis. God comes out the most frightful shit. Telling his children they can't eat the fruit of a tree he'd planted in their garden. Then condemning them to eternal punishment when they did.'

Evie said 'Well not quite eternal.'

'But no one knew that at the time. What human father would behave like that? And what human children with any spirit wouldn't behave like that – just pinching an apple!' He walked on. 'Of course some people think God wrote Genesis himself. In fact –' He stopped abruptly, so that Evie almost bumped into him. 'Perhaps it should seem that he did! Perhaps that's what I'm saying!'

'That he is or isn't a shit?'

'Perhaps he had to be thought so! That's why we wrote it like that. Then we as his children wouldn't feel too bad about being shits ourselves!'

'Why shouldn't we feel bad about being shits?'

'One sometimes has to behave like a bit of a shit to stay alive! Life's a shitty business. It might make things easier if one thought God a bit of a shit.' He thought – Was that what Lilith meant about evolution?

Evie said 'But we don't.'

'No, but we tell his story as if he is. Perhaps that's the muddle.'

'And we don't stay alive.'

'No, we have children.'

'Jesus wasn't a shit.'

Adam stopped in his walk again. Evie swerved round him. He said 'Perhaps that's it!'

'What's what?'

'Jesus seemed at home with people who were shits! I mean people who knew they were shits!'

'But it's still not good to be a shit!'

'No, that's right. That's the muddle. No, not muddle. Knot.'

Evie said 'Sophie doesn't mind us being shits.'

Adam stopped again. He said – 'That's right!' Evie went on ahead of him. He thought – Isn't there something called a love-knot? That both binds and leaves you free?

Then – It was the Old Man who realised he had a brilliant wife.

3

The Old Man's children, Adam and Eve, lie side by side in bed. Adam leans over and half on top of her. He says 'I don't think they think we know how to do this.'

Eve says 'Perhaps we don't.'

'It's worth a try.'

'It all seems a bit complex.'

She turns away, and looks out between the fronds of their shelter to where in the distance on the plains far below there are shapes of dust swirling.

Adam says 'Did he tell you how we were made?'

Eve says 'He never tells me anything.'

'He told me we're made of dust. The stuff of the universe.'

'He seems embarrassed to say that sort of thing in front of me.'

Adam looks out across Eve towards the plains where in the fields there are the shapes of figures working.

Adam says 'He's shy with women.'

'He doesn't know I've seen them in bed together.'

'What was it like?'

'He seemed to be strangling her.'

'Perhaps he was.'

'Why?'

'He doesn't want us to know that she exists.'

'But why not?'

'Perhaps he thinks then he wouldn't seem all-powerful. Perhaps it would make things a bit complex.'

'I thought they were making love.'

'Perhaps that's it.'

'What?' Eve rolls on to her back again and looks up at him.

Adam says 'He wants us to think things are all nice and easy in the Garden.'

'So we won't want to go?'

'Or so that we will.'

'Yes.' She puts up a hand and touches his cheek. She says 'I sometimes feel I'd quite like you to strangle me.'

Adam says 'I sometimes feel I'd quite like to strangle you.'

'Then why don't you?'

'Because then I'd be on my own.'

'Like he makes out he is.'

'Yes.'

Eve seems to think about this. She says 'You mean he wants to be seen to be all-powerful?'

'And you say he isn't.'

'No.'

'I suppose not if he needs her with him.'

Eve rolls away from him on to her side again. On the plain the swirls of dust are like arms reaching up to the sky.

She says 'Do you think that's why they spend so much time hanging around us in the Garden?'

'Why?'

'To see what we get up to. If it's no good.'

'And because heaven's so boring? Well, I suppose it was a gamble.'

'What was?'

'Us.'

Eve seems to think some more about this. She says 'Then shouldn't we be helping him with it?'

'With what?'

'His problem.'

Adam says 'How?'

'Well, if we're his children, we're supposed to be more evolved than he is, aren't we?'

Adam says 'You mean, we needn't seem to be on our own?'

'No.'

'All right.' Adam thinks about this. 'Try putting your hand here. I'll put my mouth there.'

Eve says 'Good heavens!'

'What?'

'It's as if something's growing out of nothing!'

Adam thinks – Perhaps that's what he called dust – the stuff of the universe.

Eve thinks – Well I'll call it a big bang.

4

Adam continued on his way to Sophie's school. He wished he was back at his computer. He thought – The next scene must be between Eve and the Serpent. But who or what is the Serpent, if Adam and Eve knew what they were doing? And why did sex come to be called a sin – because it was still thought they should expect things to be nice and easy?

– To call something a sin however means that you know you are responsible?

Adam and Evie were coming within sight of Sophie's school. It was a specialist school, catering for clever pupils hoping to get university scholarships. The headmaster was an eccentric who got into trouble both with authorities and parents; it was said he gave children too much responsibility. Lately however he was said to be suffering from a stroke; though some said this was a typical ruse to evade responsibility.

The school was in a squat modern building which looked as if the top floors had been knocked off – by a stroke (so Adam joked). There was what appeared to be a makeshift dome on the flat roof, which seemed to have been put there to make the best of a deformity. At a parents' meeting a hostile critic had likened the school to the Tower of Babel, and Adam had remarked that it was from the collapse of the Tower that humans had stopped trying to get up to heaven and had gone out to organise the world.

Now, in his walk, Adam paused by an alleyway to see if he could get any view of what was happening outside the school. Evie had gone on ahead. He could see the dome on the roof, which looked like that of an observatory.

A woman was approaching down the alleyway behind him. She stopped by his side, and she too looked up at the roof of the school. He thought he recognised her: perhaps she was the mother who had telephoned to Evie? He said 'What's happening, do you know?'

She said 'They're not saying.'

'They never do.'

'Do you think they know?'

He thought – Well yes, that's an interesting thing to say. She had a broad round face with good cheekbones. He thought – Or perhaps she is like someone in my story.

Then – I suppose it's become natural to think that scares like this might be the result of a threat of a bomb with bearded men taking hostages.

He said 'Have you got someone in the school?'

She said 'Sort of.'

He said 'It might be one of their experiments. Men with black beards taking hostages.'

She looked at him. He hoped she was thinking – That's an interesting thing to say.

Evie had stopped some way ahead. She called back – 'Are you coming?'

He called – 'Yes!'

The woman said 'See you.'

He walked on. He thought – Well that's another odd thing to say. Then – I know who she reminds me of – Lilith, in my story.

The school building stood back from the road behind a playground fronted by railings with ornamental gates. He imagined the playground as a field of fire that one might have to run across.

There were police cars and policemen in yellow flak-jackets in front of the gates. A small crowd had gathered on the pavement on the near side of the road. Evie had gone into the road and was talking to a policeman. The policeman seemed to be trying to make her go back into the crowd on the pavement.

He wondered – If the police are seen to have so much power, like the Old Man in my story, don't they come to feel guilty?

– You don't feel guilty if you love?

Evie came back from talking to the policeman. She said 'They got a phone call.'

'What did it say?'

'He won't say, and I don't suppose he knows.'

'It could be a hoax?'

Evie turned away. Adam thought – She doesn't like it when she thinks I don't take things seriously.

Then – But to say it might be a hoax is taking it seriously!

He said 'Was that woman the mother who rang you up about the school?'

'What woman?'

'The woman I was talking to.'

Evie remained turned away. He thought – I suppose it looked as if I was flirting.

He regretted not staying at home and getting on with his story about the Old Man and Lilith and the children in the Garden. But might not finding out what was happening to Sophie be part of it? They had christened her Sophie because of Sophia, or wisdom, a name for the Holy Ghost. Or rather that was what had come into his mind at the time, though perhaps not into Evie's. Evie was known as Evie because it was absurd if she was just Eve if he was Adam. He sometimes wished he wasn't called Adam, because wasn't

Christ sometimes called the second Adam? It was useful to think some things were a hoax.

The next scene he would write was somewhere in the air above his head; or at the back of his mind like the unseen dark matter of the universe that holds things together as well as making them fly apart. It would be to do with Eve rather than Evie; or Sophia rather than Sophie. But how had that woman seemed to know him?

Explanations didn't get you anywhere. That was a lesson of the Tower of Babel.

He needed to keep moving.

The road that ran in front of the railings and gates of the school curved out of sight to the right at the far end of the playground. There was a house on the corner facing down the road in his direction, that might or might not have something to do with the school. Its windows and door and sloping roof were like a man with a hat on watching him. He did not see any point in waiting outside the gates of the school. He said to Evie 'I think I'll just go and try to see what's happening.'

Evie said 'They're not letting anyone through.'

'No, I thought I'd go along on the right and see if there's any way of seeing into the garden at the back.'

'You'll get them all blown up!'

'I'll be very careful.'

'You're not going back to your computer?'

'No, I promise.' He thought – Well that's true as it stands.

He set off along the road. He thought – The trouble is, a sentence comes into your head and you can't press 'Save' and see whether to use it later. For instance – The façade of that house was like one of those American detectives who always seem to keep their hats on in the house.

– But this really hasn't got anything to do with my story.

5

The Old Man and Lilith are sitting in the Garden under their tree. They are facing at right angles to each other. Lilith says 'You'll miss them.'

The Old Man says 'Yes I know.'

'You can always give them formal advice at a later stage.'

'Which they won't follow.'

'No.'

Lilith stands and reaches up to pick a fruit from the tree. She blows on the fruit as if there might be dust on it. She licks her fingers.

The Old Man says 'What are they doing now, do you know?'

Lilith says 'Just lying about as usual, I suppose.'

'It might be more exciting for us to watch what happens when they're out.'

'Yes indeed.' She put the fruit in her pocket. 'You stay here.'

'Where are you going?'

'Just for a walk.'

The Old Man thinks – She's up to no good, I suppose.

Lilith goes to the edge of the Garden and looks over. There are the figures working in the fields below. She thinks – I mustn't let them see me.

– Or perhaps I can just be seeing how Sophie's getting on at that school?

Eve wakes up to find herself on her own in their shelter at the edge of the Garden. She thinks Adam must have gone to reconnoitre a possible escape-route over the wall. She emerges from the shelter and stands in the sunlight and stretches. At this edge of the Garden there is no wall, just the chasm. She can surely be seen by the figures working in the fields below.

She does exercises regularly, because she and Adam have so little room to move about in the Garden. She decides now to do some with her back to the chasm, bending and keeping her legs straight and touching her toes. It might then be as if a wind were blowing through her, shaking the branches of a tree.

Adam had been so gentle, their love-making had seemed to be over before it had begun.

But there are no beginnings and endings in the Garden!

Perhaps if a worker were to see her, he would climb up the cliff from the fields below and offer to show them how to get over the wall.

She remains bent over with her back to the chasm for a while; then straightens and stretches, grimacing as if in pain. What would real pain be like? Something would be happening? She put her hands behind her as if to protect her back.

Or perhaps it would be more sensible to go and chat with the Old Man, who would be sitting beneath his tree. Perhaps if she were nice enough he would allow her and Adam an excursion out of the Garden. Or for this, might she have to be nasty?

She sets off through a grove of olive trees, and pauses by one to pick a fruit from a bough. She is biting into it when she hears someone coming up behind her. She thinks she might say to the Old Man – Oh dear, I thought it might be one of those workers from the plain! Then when she turns there indeed is one of them! Gnarled and knobbly like the root of a tree. But with a funny piece of cloth around his loins. She wonders – Does the Old Man have a piece of cloth like that under his robe?

The worker says 'You were told you weren't allowed to eat the fruit of that tree!'

Eve says 'Oh was I? Who told you that?'

'A lady on the cliff-face. She was climbing down. She told me to climb up and tell you.'

'Oh really?'

She thinks – Why not just say you saw me doing my exercises!

He says 'She says then you can be punished.'

'And what would be the point of that?'

'You'd feel better. More free.'

He smiles at her. She thinks – You mean, I wouldn't have an obligation?

He says 'Isn't that what you want?'

'I don't know. Is it?'

'Yes.'

She walks on. She has her back to him. She thinks – Perhaps he isn't really there. Perhaps he was in my imagination.

Adam had said to her – When you can imagine things, that is what it might mean to be free!

She puts a hand to her head to see if it is there.

She thinks – But I was on my way to see the Old Man beneath the tree.

6

Adam had set off along the pavement on the near side of the road in front of Sophie's school, towards the house that faced him on the corner on the right. He walked as if nonchalantly, because he thought that, like this, there would be less chance of anyone stopping him. He wanted to let his mind go back to where it had been before the presumed bomb-scare at Sophie's school – to the story of God and Adam and Eve in the Garden of Eden. Were there connections? Snatches of what might be his next few pages fluttered in the air just above his head; if he grabbed at them he would lose them, but he did not want them to fly away. He had left his wife Evie in the small crowd being held back across the road facing the school; it was right for her to stay to see how things turned out along ordinary lines of communication. He wanted to get a view of what was happening from the side or round the back.

He stumbled slightly, brushing against a wall. He thought – I must appear vague enough not to pose a threat, but not so half-witted that I might have to be apprehended anyway. So is this an experiment to see whether by one's attitude and attention one can affect what happens? Of course I am anxious to see if my daughter Sophie is all right! I am going to the house on the corner to see if there is a way round to the back of the school.

The house he was approaching had a low wooden gate leading to a small front garden. Approaching it from the other direction, from where the road curved round to the right, was the figure of a woman who seemed also to be heading for the house. She reached the gate just ahead of him; then turned and faced him. She was the woman, yes, with whom he had spoken a short time ago in the street. She had said – See you! He looked back the way he had come to see if Evie was watching him; it might appear indeed that he and this woman had been flirting. But he could not make out Evie in the crowd. He turned back to the woman who was waiting by the garden gate. He said 'How did you get here?' She said 'I stay here.'

He began to articulate in his mind – I mean – But then he did not know what he meant.

She said – 'Would you like to come in?'

He said 'Thank you.'

He followed her through the gate and up the short garden path. Watching her movements as she walked he thought – It is some-times more grown-up to prefer the back view to the front?

She said 'Did you find out any more about what's going on?'

He said 'No. They had a telephone call.'

'They may want the publicity.'

'For a sense of identity?'

'In the next world, if not this.'

He wondered – Is this a grown-up conversation?

She had a key to the front door of the house. He followed her in. He thought – Might we really go straight upstairs to the bedroom?

– Or might there be CCTV cameras at every corner; men in darkened rooms somewhere spending their lives watching screens.

They went past a door to a kitchen/dining-room and then the bottom of a staircase. At the back there was a conservatory beyond which there could be seen the greenery of a garden. He thought – Yes this is what I am supposed to be looking for.

There was an old man in a wheelchair in the conservatory. He had white hair floating down beneath a panama hat. The woman said 'I've brought someone to see you.'

The old man said 'Who?'

'He's got a daughter in the school.'

'What's her name.'

Adam said 'Sophie.'

'Let me see you.'

Adam thought – He's the headmaster who's had a stroke?

– Or is he that man I had a discussion with on the radio?

The old man said 'You're that fellow who believes in chance. Free will. You don't think they're contradiction.'

Adam said 'No.'

'Why not?'

'Chance gives you the freedom to take advantage of it or not.'

'That doesn't make sense.'

'No.'

Adam thought – This is a grown-up conversation!

The woman said to the old man 'He wants to try to see what's going on in the school from the back.'

Adam thought – But I didn't tell her that!

The old man said 'And what do you think is going on?'

Adam said 'And you're the person who thinks that everything's determined by our genes and DNA.'

'It's necessary to believe that.'

'Why?'

'Or everything's out of control.'

Adam thought – You want things to be in control?

As if he had heard this, the old man said 'Yes.'

Adam thought – You could be in a story of some old God who has retired and is sitting in a deck-chair watching the sea.

He looked round. He thought – But it would be possible, yes, to write a true purely factual description of this place – the conservatory with its potted palm tree and its sloping glass roof, the old man with his panama hat and his air of his job being over and done. This would convey information of a sort. But what would have been learnt?

The woman said 'Wasn't there something you wanted to ask him?'

Adam thought he might say – No, it was you I wanted to meet.

He said to the old man 'What's real still makes a story. The point is what we can learn.'

The old man did not seem to hear this. He said 'You'd like to see out at the back?'

'Yes please.'

'She'll show you.'

Adam followed the woman through glass doors to an area that was less like a garden than an orchard. Adam thought – This is absurd.

When they were walking through rough grass and between fruit trees he said 'Did I tell you that I wanted to get round the back?'

She said 'I don't know, didn't you? It seemed to me that that was what you would want.'

'I'm writing a story about Adam and Eve and the Garden.'

'Yes your daughter Sophie told me.'

'You know Sophie?'

'I've been teaching her.'

She led him to where there was a wall overgrown with ivy. It seemed, yes, that this wall should separate the garden of the house from the garden of the school at the back. He thought – I must try to remember details of this, even if I don't understand what they mean.

He said 'We like to make God a bit of a monster, so that we can be a bit monstrous ourselves.'

'Which he isn't. And which we needn't be.'

'No. And that's our true original sin.'

They had come to a place in the orchard where there was a tree with a branch that stretched over the wall. She said 'This is where the children climb in when they want to pinch the fruit.' Then she put a hand on his arm and her head against his shoulder, and laughed. She said 'I'm sorry!'

He said 'Oh that's all right.' Then quickly – 'You mean I can get over here into the garden of the school?'

'If you wish.'

He thought – But the children were supposed not to have been able to get back in?

He said 'Could you give me a hand up?'

He reached with his hands towards the branch of the tree. The woman stood with her back against the trunk and cupped her hands in front of her. It was as if she were an acrobat and about to toss a fellow acrobat high into the air. He said 'Are you sure?' She said 'No not at all.' He put a foot into her hands and tried to stand, at the same time to get a grip with his fingers on the trunk of the tree. He thought – And my foot is against your groin and my groin will be against your face. He made a grab for the horizontal branch and got his hands round it. He said 'Mind I don't kick you.' She said 'Never mind.' He got his feet clear of her and scrabbled with them on the trunk; then pulled with his arms and swung a leg over the branch and hung upside down like a sloth. She said 'Are you all right?' He said 'I'm fine.' She said 'Will you be able to get down the other side?' He said 'No problem.' He heaved and scraped and got himself round on top of the branch like a leopard. She said 'Well I think I'd better get back to let him know what's happening.' He said 'Who are you?' She said 'I keep an eye on him.' He said 'But I mean –' She said 'Oh well, I'm the science mistress, and he's the old history master.' He said 'Oh I see.' He thought – And yes, I see why you are laughing. He pulled himself along the branch of the tree to where it stretched beyond the wall. He thought – You mean, we do things because they appear to be the right things to do, and we make up reasons and explanations later. He thought he might call back – See you! – but he did not think this would be necessary.

7

Eve comes upon the Old Man sitting beneath his tree. She says 'Don't you ever get bored just sitting here in your garden?'

He seems to convey at the same time both – 'Yes' – and – 'Not with you around!'

He smiles and rearranges the robe across his lap.

She says to herself – He doesn't know that I know about what he gets up to with Lilith!

She says 'I'm bored. I've got nothing to do all day. Can't we play a game or something?'

He says 'What do you suggest?'

'Well, you could tell me not to do something, and then I could do it.'

'What would be the point of that?'

'Then you could punish me.'

'And what would be the point of that?'

'Then I wouldn't feel so helpless. So goody-goody. Such a worm.'

She sits down beside him. She thinks – And I might get to know what you've got under that robe!

He says 'Who have you been talking to?'

'Well, one of your workers came up from the plains. Or he might have been in my imagination. Do you do imagination?'

'I'm not supposed to. I'm supposed to do reality.'

'This person said he'd been talking to a lady on the cliff-face.'

'Oh dear, now I wonder who that could be!'

'He said she'd said you'd said that I couldn't eat the fruit of a tree.'

'Now why should I do that?'

'I suppose, because if we did, Adam and I might not feel so stuck. I mean, if you were angry, we might have a grievance, and not feel so obliged. Then we might be able to get out of the Garden.'

'Is that what you want?'

'Well, if you didn't want to keep us.'

'But I like having you here.'

'We could still keep in touch with you.'

The Old Man is thinking – She is much prettier now she is growing up.

Eve is thinking – All right, this is a game!

She says 'But don't you think we ought to go?'

'I suppose so.'

'Well then, we've all got the problem. We both want to do things and don't.'

'So what do you suggest?'

Eve makes out she is considering this. She thinks – That worker from the plains, he looked nasty, but nice and nasty at the same time, do you think?

– That's one way out of a predicament!

She says 'Well, supposing you as well as we did something that you knew was wrong, like getting us to do something silly and then punishing us, then you wouldn't feel so bad about us leaving the Garden.'

'But I'd feel bad about myself.'

'Well, you could make it up to us later.'

'How?'

'Well, we could work on that when then time comes.'

The Old Man adjusts the robe across his lap. He thinks – Ah yes. And what I am now thinking is – What if we had a child!

He says 'But now, what do you suggest?'

Eve says 'Well, what if I sit on your lap for instance.'

'Then I could punish you?'

'Sort of. If you wish. And I could say I'm sorry.'

'And you mean I might feel sorry?'

'Well, when the time comes. And you'd feel a bit more free.'

The Old Man thinks – And we'd have had it all ways up and down and sideways at the same time?

He says 'It might all get a bit out of control sometimes.'

'Then that would be exciting!'

'You think so?'

'Well, something would be happening!'

He says 'All right, come on then, you'd better sit on my knee.'

8

When Adam and Evie had gone with Sophie to have a look at what might become her school, Adam had at first not wanted her to go there. The playground had represented his worst imaginings of Babel after the collapse of the Tower – children moving aimlessly to and fro with mobile phones or connections from iPods pressed to their ears. They were intent on whatever waves were being pumped into their brains by machinery, their eyes appearing to attend to nothing that was happening in the world around them. Occasionally as if by instinct they would dart out a foot or a hand to try to trip someone up or to seize an iPod or a phone, and the victim would fall to the ground and writhe there like a footballer. And then the instrument, if gained, would be thrown from one to another while the owner lurched after it, until this activity for no apparent reason suddenly ceased, and the children were once more cocooned within ghostly noises enfolding them from anywhere or nowhere.

Adam had said 'We can't leave her here!'

Evie had said 'Life's like this now.'

Then Sophie had said 'But they're playing a game!'

Adam had said 'What game?'

Sophie had said 'They're saying – Look, we're showing you that we know it's all so silly!'

So Adam and Evie had eventually agreed that Sophie should go to the school, mainly because Sophie said she wanted to, and because the headmaster had written a booklet in which he said that children anyway learned for themselves what they thought was worth learning, and could best be guided by being trusted.

Adam had thought – Dear God, and you wait to see if either that works or it doesn't?

And now, stretched along the branch of a tree in the position of a ruminating leopard, Adam wondered – Are we now to be guided by putting our trust in the instincts of children?

Then – But was that old man in the house really the headmaster or history master? And was the woman really the science mistress? Well, why shouldn't they be? And what is the point of 'really'?

When he looked down from the branch he saw that he was now, yes, beyond the wall and above the garden at the back of the school. He thought – I surely don't have to go on reassuring myself about what on earth I am doing.

Beneath him was an area of mounds and excavations like a mock-up of an archaeological dig. He wondered – What lesson have they been doing here – History? Anthropology? Beyond this there was an enclosure like that of a miniature zoo, containing just one sheep and one goat. He thought – Biology? Religion?

Ahead, over a slight rise, there was what looked like the top of a small blue tent. Adam had got himself as far as he could along the branch of the tree; but if he dropped to the ground now, he might land in one of the opened-up graves and thus disturb whatever was their exercise or experiment. And indeed, from the ground, he might never be able to climb back on to the branch again, and so might be taken hostage with the rest of them, or whatever the joke was – and there he would be in an already-dug grave.

Might not 'reality' be just when things were seen as funny?

If he stood on the branch, he might be able to see who or what was inside the tent. Of course it might be just children having set up an encampment.

Then unexpectedly – What for God's sake had been the implications of Eve sitting on the Old Man's knee?

– Oh yes, the Old Man was letting himself be implicated in the so-called Fall.

Adam twisted his head to see if there was any branch on a higher level that if he stood he might hold on to to stop himself falling. But in so turning his head he lost his grip on the branch to which he had been clinging, and he slipped round and was once more hanging upside down like a sloth.

He wondered – What part did sloths play in evolution?

It seemed that there was now no other possibility than for him to let go of the branch with his legs, and then with his arms, and drop down on to a small mound of earth from a newly-dug grave that happened (what indeed was chance) to be just underneath him. He thought – And why should dug earth not be seen as cultivation rather than a grave?

He dropped down and crouched with his fingers lightly on the mound, on which there were growing a few wild grasses. Just in front of his eyes there was a thin stalk with a seed-pod at the top which had wings like those of an insect. He thought – I have not seen anything like this before! But then, why should I? He could blow on it to see if it would fly.

He smiled. He imagined a conversation about this with his daughter Sophie; or perhaps with the science mistress.

He thought he should make his way round, or over, the stem of grass without disturbing it. This seemed important. There was a story that when archaeologists had opened up one of the tombs in the Egyptian Valley of the Kings, the inrush of air had caused all the painting that had been on the walls for thousands of years to disappear in a flash and for ever. But there might have been just enough time for the illumination to have entered into the minds of one or two of the men who had been unwitting instruments of destruction, and to have been preserved there?

So he had to be careful.

He straightened his legs, and moved round both the seed and the grave with his hands on the ground like a monkey. When he was clear, he stood upright and walked to the top of the last mound in the configuration from which he could see the whole of the small tent which was of the size for two people to sleep in.

The flaps at the front were tied back. Within were three girls, of an age perhaps to be in their last year at school, seated cross-legged on the ground around a square of cloth; they had their eyes closed as if they were concentrating. One of them was his daughter Sophie. Adam thought – I know what they are doing! Or at least this reminds me of a story I once told Sophie.

There had been an incident in his own youth during a country-house weekend when he and some friends had played a trick upon an opinionated acquaintance who had been ridiculing any idea of the possibility of extra-sensory perception. So Adam and his friends, one evening when they had all been somewhat drunk, had told this acquaintance that they would give him a demonstration of how he himself could become imbued with such a faculty. They would shuffle a pack of cards and he would cut it and place it face down on the table. Then they would all close their eyes and concentrate or empty their minds (the same thing?) on whatever might be the unseen card at the top of the pack, so that the acquaintance would be enabled to name it correctly. The trick had been – how on earth had they got away with it? they must have all been very drunk! – the trick had been that one of Adam's friends had an identical pack of cards so that by the time the potential victim named the top card – and after they had managed to keep him with his eyes closed for a few moments longer by saying – Are you sure? Are you absolutely sure? – the accomplice had managed to find the required card in the identical pack and had placed it on the top of the pack on the table. So that when the acquaintance opened his eyes and turned up this card it was – lo and behold! – the one that he had nominated. They repeated the trick once, to confirm his dawning suspension of disbelief; then said that they should not challenge any further what might be called the fates.

But the point of Adam's story and memory had been – the next morning, when both he and the acquaintance were sober, the acquaintance had come to him and said he had been so struck by the amazing events of the night before that he had come to him, Adam, in the sober morning, for just one more confirmation: so could Adam please just perform the apparent miracle with him once again. But Adam was now on his own with no accomplice, so there was no chance of the trick being repeated. But he agreed to go through the motions of it, because he would feel somewhat guilty if the victim's illusions were not finally dispelled. But then – and this was the punch line of the story – the next morning when just the two of them went through the performance again – lo and behold it did still work! That is – the card turned up now literally at random was the one nominated by the former sceptic – and with no chicanery. And so the sceptic's faith had been confirmed rather than dispelled. And Adam's comment when he had told the story to Sophie had been – You see, he had believed it would work, and so it did.

Sophie had said – But what did you believe?

He had said – I try not to believe or disbelieve. I try to take note of what happens.

He had thought – Pompous, but true.

Now, watching the three girls in the tent, he saw Sophie open her eyes and smile, and then slowly turn her head and look at him. After a time she widened her eyes and said 'You!'

He thought he should say – I came over the wall on that tree.

Sophie said 'We were doing that experiment!'

'The one with the cards?'

'No, no cards. Just concentrating or making your mind a blank, and seeing what turns up.'

'And something turns up.'

'Which happens to be you.'

The other girls were now watching him with interest. Sophie said 'This is Aisha, this is Amelie. And this is my father.'

Adam said 'Hi.'

The girls said 'Hi.'

Sophie said 'I'm sorry, I never know if I pronounce your name right.'

Adam said 'Adam.'

Sophie said 'I mean Aisha.'

They all got giggles for a moment.

Adam squatted down outside the tent. He thought – This is the cavern on the walls of which just for an instant there are exquisite paintings which might illuminate the meaning of the universe, but then they disappear forever unless someone has absorbed them.

He said 'What's happening in the school?'

One of the girls said as if she were an actor showing distaste for a bad script – 'There's a complete stand-off between hostage-takers and their victims.'

Adam said 'And what are their demands?'

The other girl said 'Complete change in human nature in forty minutes.' Then she seemed on the point of giggles.

Adam said 'I see.'

The first girl said 'Complete probity, sanity, and integrity all round.'

Adam said 'And what if these demands aren't met?'

The second girl said looking at Sophie – 'Flood? Bird flu? Nuclear annihilation?'

Sophie said brusquely 'Something like that.'

Adam sat cross-legged on the ground. He thought – All right, so the world's a stage. So what's the reality?

He said 'How long have you been here?'

One of the girls said 'Forty minutes?' They seemed to move rapidly between hilarity and solemnity like the sun on a twirling mirror.

He thought – Of course, if I have done my job right, Sophie will have learned how to deal with such things better that me! He said 'Where's the rest of the school?'

'They were given the day off.'

'And who telephoned the police?'

'Well we didn't.'

'I've been talking to the old man next door.'

'Perhaps it was him!'

'Who's the woman with him? She says she's the science mistress.'

Sophie seemed to draw with her finger on the ground.

Adam thought of saying – You're wanting to demonstrate that almost all such drama, such craziness, has no substance, no point? You want to see what would happen if people saw this –

– But that's what you can't say?

Sophie stood up and said in a matter-of-fact way – 'It looks as if there's a complete stand-off between fundamentalists, dogmatists of all sorts, and people who watch and listen.'

Adam said 'And you as experimenters – you learn from the experiment?'

'We'll have to see.'

'And who chooses you?'

'Luck? Desperation? Presumption?' Then briskly again – 'Would you like to see round the school?'

He said 'Yes please.'

Sophie set off down a grassy slope towards the back of the school building. He followed her. He thought – I can explain to Evie that I am writing this as a story – a story being that which can tell something vital that can be told in no better way.

– Children by their coming into being are both God and human. How can one say this?

The back entrance to the school was up two flights of steps that rose from opposite directions and met at the top like the apex to a triangle. At the base there were shallow steps going down what seemed to be the entrance to a basement.

He said 'So what's the experiment.'

Sophie said 'Two masked men broke into assembly this morning.'

'I see.'

'They took their hostages into the gym in the basement, because that's where there are water and toilets.'

'Good heavens!'

'But we weren't in the basement. We'd wanted to get out into the air.'

He thought – So some things do, as well as some things don't, have meaning?

He said 'And that's all?'

'The rest of the people can make of this what they like.'

They had come to the steps up into the school. Sophie led the way to double doors at the top which opened onto a long stone-flagged corridor with doors on either side which presumably led into classrooms. The place appeared to be deserted. Adam thought – It looks as if it's hardly been used for some time.

Sophie said 'On this floor we did History, Languages, Sociology, and Media Studies.'

Adam thought it would be unnecessary to say – Which are subjects that are not verified or falsified, so people can make of them what they like.

Sophie said 'Mathematics and Science were in the basement.'

He said 'Why did you have to get out?'

'It became too stuffy. We couldn't see out.'

He thought – You could verify or falsify what you liked?

He said 'And what happens on the floors above this?'

'They've been left empty since the top of the building was knocked off.'

He thought – By a storm? By a bombardment?

She said 'It was terrible! All the pipes burst!'

He said 'You mean if men with masks and black beards didn't exist, we'd have to invent them?'

She said 'Something like that. But why?'

He said 'Well, I suppose we want to find reasons for things that are not in our control.'

'You mean then we think they might be?'

'Yes.'

Sophie opened a door into a classroom on the left. Adam thought – There may be a window through which I will be able to see over the wall into the garden of the house of the old man and the woman next door. I don't yet quite know who they are.

Sophie said 'The science mistress thinks she knows you.'

'Oh does she?'

'Though she doesn't think you remember her.'

'Oh but I did!'

'Where did you meet her?'

'On my way to the school.'

He thought – Oh yes, she was someone who seems able to be in two places at once.

In the classroom there were rows of old-fashioned desks-and-seats all in one, as if they were stocks for the detention of wrong-doers. Confronting them was a dais with a larger table-desk and a separate chair. He thought – But the aloofness of authority was some sort of entrapment.

He said 'And what did you learn here?'

She said 'The boys hid their mobiles under their desks and watched pornography.'

'And so you learned – '

'To have feeling without meaning.'

There was a window at the far end of the room. He went to it and looked out. He could see only bits of the roof of the house over the wall.

He said 'But you were doing experiments in the basement.'

She said 'Yes, but we couldn't see the effects of them outside.'

He wondered – Did you build the observatory?

He turned away from the window. He said 'Can you get up to the higher floors?'

'Yes, but they're not considered safe.'

'I might be able to see over the wall.'

'Do you want to?'

He thought – I suppose I do have some reason.

She said 'Well, we could try.'

He went back to the door. He did not watch to see if she was following him. He thought – I suppose I like to have my own show of confidence. Then when he was in the stone-flagged corridor and he saw that she was with him, he said 'I can't really do this.'

She said 'I think you're doing brilliantly!'

'I was brought up by people like your boring history master.'

'He used to be the headmaster.'

'Yes.'

He went to the bottom of the flight of stairs that went up in a rectangular spiral to the floor above. He thought – I should have taken more note of the style and trappings of that classroom, I may not go there again.

He went up the stairs with Sophie following him. He said 'Why do they think these upper stories are unsafe?'

She said 'I suppose because they want to.'

'They got damaged by a bomb?'

'Oh yes, there was a bomb.'

'They were being used for observation?'

'Yes, but not for experiment.'

'There could have been experiment?'

'About killing and maiming? Destroying the enemy?'

'Well, seeing what happens.'

He thought – I suppose any experiment is something of a hazard.

They had come to a landing similar to the one they had left. They went through a door into a classroom directly above, and similar to, the one in which they had been on the floor below – except that this room had no furniture, and smelt of paint.

He said 'You don't feel deprived?'

She said 'Deprived? No, nor particularly blessed!' She laughed.

'I mean, you're not sorry we didn't send you to an ordinary school?'

She said 'Good heavens, weren't you trying to educate me your-selves?'

He thought – Perhaps this is the level on which we are off-stage.

He went to the window at the end of the room and looked out. He now could see over the wall down into the garden of the house next door. The roof of the conservatory was in view, but neither the old man nor the woman.

He said 'I'm so grateful.'

She said 'Who to? What for?'

He thought he should say – To you – but didn't.

There was the faint sound of breaking glass from somewhere below.

She said 'They'll be getting in soon.'

He said 'And then what will you tell them?'

'What would you want to hear?'

'That very little of what appears to be happening matters.'

'But we don't quite know what does matter.'

'Well not exactly.'

The sounds were of people breaking in at the front door of the building. Sophie went back into the passage. He followed her. They stood looking down the well of the staircase.

He said 'But shouldn't we be going?'

She said 'You're in charge.'

'I'm in charge!'

'Oh all right.' She set off ahead of him down the stairs. She said looking back 'Just so long as we get out of this place!'

9

The Old Man said 'What on earth are they up to?'

Lilith said 'They have to be doing something.'

'But they're not really doing anything.'

'Would you rather they just did?'

'What – '

'Evil.'

'Why evil?'

'Because that's what seems to keep freedom available. Evolution turning.'

'And they chose it?'

'And you let them.'

'I didn't tell them.'

'But I know what you got up to with Eve.'

'You don't.'

'I do.'

'Anyway you fixed it.'

'She'd seen what we got up to.'

'She didn't.'

'She did.'

'And this is what things are like now?'

'This sort of thing. But it's their job to see it's silly.'

The Old Man was sitting in a deckchair looking out into space as if it were a distant sea. Lilith was lying on the grass beside him with a sun-hat over her eyes.

The Old Man said 'I sometimes can hardly remember how we began all this.'

Lilith said 'We wanted something except ourselves to be able to grow up. To be responsible. They had to have the chance to go wrong or else they wouldn't be free.'

'Free of us?'

'Yes.'

'But they're not.'

'No. So no wonder it's all a bit difficult.'

The Old Man moved restlessly. He wished he had some of that stuff with him that blocked out the sun.

He said 'I should have wiped them out when I had the chance.'

'You don't mean that.'

'No I don't. It's just something I say when I feel guilty.'

'Does it help?'

'No.'

'Well perhaps they'll learn that too.'

Lilith sat up and put her hands round her knees. She looked out over space. She thought she might go for a swim.

The Old Man said 'And anyway, without a bit of risk, there soon wouldn't have been enough room.'

'Not after what you got up to with Eve.'

'There you go again!' The Old Man looked gratified. He said 'They had to be given a pattern, as well as the chance of change. Or they wouldn't have known what to trust.'

'Nor would you.'

'You think I've changed?'

'Why else were you up with Eve?'

'You mean that fellow on the motor-bike?'

'What fellow on the motor-bike?'

'Oh never mind.' The Old Man put his panama hat over his eyes and appeared to go to sleep.

Lilith looked at him as if amused. She said 'So you're feeling better now?'

He said 'Yes.'

'Then I hope they are too.'

The Old Man, as if he were talking through his hat, said – 'I did have the idea that instead of just letting them get on with risking chance, there could be a group or groups programmed to show them the odds.'

'Programmed how to do chance?'

'Yes.'

'Well that's a contradiction.'

'Don't I do contradictions?'

'Yes. But groups fight. Individuals can learn to be at peace.'

'Well, it was worth a try.'

'Sophie says it has to be individuals.'

'Sophie?'

'Sorry, Sophia.'

'All right.' The Old Man appeared to be going contentedly to sleep.

'Lilith said 'Well I'm going for a swim.'

'Mind you don't go over the cliff.'

'That's exactly what I'm going to do.'

'Well have a nice day.'

'That's what you should be doing.'

'Going over the cliff?'

'Yes.'

'I'm leaving that to the chap on the motor-bike.'

'Who is this chap on the motor-bike?'

'He does the most amazing tricks. Leaps. Chances. Coincidences.'

'Did you know him with Eve?'

'Yes.'

'Well I think you might let a little more chance in with science, mathematics.'

'Oh yes I'm doing that too.'

'Does he know Sophia?'

'Who? The chap on the motor-bike? Yes, he knows Sophie.'

10

Adam followed Sophie down the staircase of the school towards the ground floor. There were the sounds of voices, of orders being shouted, at the end of the long corridor which led to the entrance at the front. He thought – But they might shoot? He said 'But what about the people in the basement?'

Sophie said 'I told you, there's no one in the basement.'

'No?'

'We went out to the tent at the back.'

'And where are the others?'

'I told you. They've all gone on a trip.'

He thought – All right, I just wanted to make sure.

When he and Sophie reached the final turn in the staircase beyond which they would become visible to anyone in the ground floor corridor, he said 'Lean against me.' He put his arm around her and she rested her head against his shoulder. They went on down the stairs. There were figures in yellow flak-jackets at the far end of the corridor; some pressed against walls. He thought – One story might be that the flak-jackets were to protect them from friendly fire.

He glanced round as if anxiously back up the stairs. Then looking ahead he said loudly 'There's no one there!' He thought – Well we've got to be saying or doing something. Then he used the hand that was not holding Sophie to make chopping gestures to his front, as if to say – Let us through! Quick! Men with masks and black beards may be coming up behind us!

Rather than – Stop us if you like, but we are people trying to make a difference to the human race.

Sophie lifted her head and exclaimed – 'They've got my mobile!'

He said 'Don't worry, I'll get it.'

She said 'It's in the tent.'

He thought – The tent? The text?

– You mean, when I've left you, I can go round the side of the building and let those girls know what's happening at the front?

– Which I shall be glad to do, because they were rather attractive.

When he and Sophie reached the door at the end of the corridor which led out into the playground, they had not been stopped nor molested, and there were now not only police but photographers and even a film crew just beyond the steps. The small crowd of onlookers was still being held back at the far side of the road. Sophie murmured 'Keep going.' He went down the steps still with his arm round her, and with Sophie keeping her face pressed against his shoulder as if hiding it from photographers. People approached them but he waved them back. He could see Evie just beyond the gates. She was standing with her arms folded and looking angry rather than upset. He thought – Good, she got them to let her come to the gates. He and Sophie had got across the playground and the gates were opened for them and Evie held her arms out. He thought he remembered – Didn't I tell her she was brilliant? He let go of Sophie and Evie took her and he said to Evie 'Get her home.' An ambulance woman came up to them but Evie said 'The last thing she wants is a fucking paramedic!' Adam thought – How on earth has she learned? Evie led Sophie away across the road. They moved through the small crowd which made way for them; then went out of sight down the street that led to their home.

Adam thought – I mustn't stop. It's when one is still that there is room for self-questioning.

– Sophie's mobile is in the tent?

– And then perhaps I can disappear back over the wall.

He set off at a jogging run down the side of the school. He thought – How did Sophie pick those two girls; was that by chance? And the rest of the school– what sort of expedition could they be on: to Madame Tussauds? another planet? He came to where he could see the branch of the tree that stretched over the wall from the garden of the house next door. He thought – Oh yes, but how do I get up on to the branch? And do I need to? The girls might help me?

– Might it be one of the points of this rigmarole, that we should become better acquainted?

He was setting off in the direction of the tent when a voice behind him said 'Hi!'

He said 'Hi.'

The two girls were standing in a lean-to shed against the garden wall just beyond the branch of the tree. He thought – It is where tools might be kept.

He said 'Sophie left her mobile.'

One of the girls said 'Yes we've got it. Here.' She handed it to him. The other girl said 'We wondered if you could possibly give us a hand up over the wall.'

He said 'Of course.'

'We don't want to be seen.'

'No.'

'Is Sophie all right?'

'She's fine.'

'How lucky that you came back!'

'Yes isn't it.'

The girls smiled. They had come and joined him beneath the branch of the tree.

One or the other of them said 'We used to be able to go to and fro from here.'

Adam said 'Yes, the science mistress told me.'

They all seemed to be on the point of laughter.

Adam thought – Where do you come from: you are foreign? Yet you don't seem foreign!

One of the girls said 'There used to be a ladder.'

Adam said 'And now it's gone?'

'So we can help each other.'

'Yes.' They were watching him. He said 'When I got up onto the branch on the other side the science mistress made a cup with her hands in front of her.'

One of the girls said 'But how will you get back?'

He said 'I don't have to. I can just have been getting Sophie her mobile phone.'

They laughed.

He made a cup of his hands in front of him as the science mistress had done, and waited for one of the girls to put her foot in it. He thought – And I will have a chance to put my arms around their thighs, and their bodies will be pressed against my face.

When the first girl was clear of him he looked up and she was on the branch above him like a leopard. She said 'Thank you.'

He thought – And now we will recognise one another.

The other girl had come up to him. She said 'Will you be all right?'

He said 'Yes I'll be fine. But what about you?'

She said 'We'll be in touch with Sophie.' Then – 'By mobile phone!' She laughed.

He cupped his hands in front of him, and the experience was repeated – of his hoisting her up to heaven and himself being left on earth as if he had just been born. The first girl was looking back from beyond the wall. She said 'See you then.' He said 'See you.' The second girl joined her. He thought – Oh well, there is some story for a mobile phone.

11

Adam stared at what he had written on his computer. He thought – My God, I am making them all so witty and sophisticated, like a nineteen-forties film!

– What was that one – *The Thin Man*? Or didn't those films really exist?

– But I mean – What about the wars, the torture, the catastrophes, that flourished then and still flourish in all parts of the world? They are accepted because it is felt they make room for new generations?

– Life evolves, but does it become much different?

Adam had recently been watching nature programmes on television. In these, fish and insects gobbled one another up; tongues darted out and snatched victims, then there was a pause while small heads looked demurely out of hugely stretched mouths. The victims did not seem to mind; it was as if they might indeed be returning peacefully to a womb. Lions ate the entrails of deer while the deer looked away like someone bored with sex. But then, if this way of seeing things was acceptable, why should not life go on much the same?

Then there was a news programme in which a soldier pulled back the head of a prisoner by the hair and looked as if he were about to pee in his mouth. Adam wondered – But where have I seen such an image before?

It was some years since he had bothered to bring up pornography on the Net, and nowadays there were stories of police software specialists on the prowl with the power to pick up (could this be true?) people whose fantasies did or did not match their own. And then – wham! a piss in the mouth would seem like nectar.

But now Adam could surely truthfully say that he was entering such dark alleyways for the sake of research – to inquire into the surely worthwhile question of what might be the springs of humans' so questionable behaviour. And why should not research have a fascination?

He tapped into the appropriate slot on the screen what he thought might be appropriate words to summon his line of enquiry; then waited while flashes of advertising appeared and disappeared like wasps in and out of a hole. Eventually he was admitted into what looked like the long corridor of a prison, in which there were peepholes through the doors to the goings-on in various cells. Then a few more clicks and he was through to a full-cell enlargement.

A naked man was lying with his back arched above a table. A metal clamp was fastened tightly round his scrotum close to his penis so that his testicles bulged as if about to burst. A cord went up from the clamp to a pulley on the ceiling, then round this and down to where from it there hung a pan like one on which weights are placed in a balance. There were already a number of weights in the pan; two naked women stood by and seemed to be considering whether to add more. The man seemed to be in a state of extreme pain or ecstasy. Adam thought – You mean, you are aiming for a state in which you can't tell the difference? The women seemed to be waiting for instructions from the man to add more weights to the pan. And the experiment would be to see if he might have an apocalyptic orgasm at the very last moment before, or perhaps even coincidental with, his balls being torn off.

– But the latter would surely be a technical impossibility. Or maybe mystically an ultimate beatification?

Then – My God, I must tell Evie!

He dallied a bit longer in dungeons where men were being racked, whipped, crucified, pissed on for pleasure. He wondered – But is this an incitement to, or a substitute for, something like starting a war in the Middle East, or making a speech in the House of Commons?

He switched off the computer. He watched the screen while it went through the motions of seeming to swallow its own sick.

He wondered – I mean if you were a young man hoping to trust in probity, morals, God, and then you saw this stuff on the Net, might you not need to go out and blow yourself up as well as other representatives of the human race?

– If you did not want to risk, that is, the apotheosis of having your balls torn off?

He went downstairs to where Evie should be having her afternoon lie-down. He sat on the edge of their bed, not quite managing to avoid her legs. He said 'Do you know what sort of porn they show nowadays on the Net?'

She said 'No, and I don't want to hear it if you do.'

'It's all about men seeming to need to be tortured and humiliated by women.'

'Well however much you may think you need it, I'm not going to torture or humiliate you.'

'But why don't people talk about it?'

'I don't know. Should they?'

'It seems so popular! And there's nothing about women being humiliated by men.'

'Perhaps you haven't looked.'

'Yes that's true.'

'Or perhaps it's so common there's no demand for it on the Net.'

He shifted his position slightly, but she did not move her legs.

He said 'I'm trying to write about all the appalling savagery that goes on that's supposed to be political, rational, purposive; and all the time maybe it's just genes, instinct, evolution, sex.'

'Well, is it?'

'I don't know.'

'Are Sophie and I still coming into what you're writing now?'

'You could be seen as characters in a story.'

'I thought it was an allegory about God and Adam and Eve.'

'But an allegory should be a way of trying to see what's going on behind words and scenes.'

'Does that need an allegory?'

'Yes, because we cover up what's going on. Or distance it as if it's on stage. And so then we don't feel responsible. And we call the cover-up reality.'

'And what do we call the allegory?'

'We might see it as a recognition of both the cover-up and the off-stage reality.'

'What is the off-stage reality?'

'I don't know. There was this chap on the Net having his balls torn off. And seeming to want it or need it. But the interesting question, surely, was – could he in fact have his apocalyptic orgasm if his balls were off?'

'You're sitting on my legs.'

'Sorry.'

'Well, could he?'

'I suppose that's the sort of thing you can't know.'

Adam shifted his weight. He thought – I lose her when I go on like this. She slips away like hands that might be holding on to the edge of a lifeboat. But don't we need a lifeboat if human nature is in the throes of shipwreck?

He said 'I think it's the way we might be seeing things from off-stage that's the reality. Both the carry-on and the cover-up are on-stage, even if the carry-on isn't talked about much. But there does seem to be a sort of off-stage availability that can assess both the carry-on and the cover-up, even if this is a bit superhuman. But humans do feel they have a bit that's superhuman too. I mean fairy stories are ways of telling of terrible things happening, which seem quite jolly.'

Evie said nothing.

He said 'Do you think it's something like this that Sophie and her friends are on about?'

'I don't know.' Then – 'Haven't you talked to Sophie and her friends?'

'Yes.'

He thought – But I've still got to get the outcome of this in my story.

He put a hand on the bedclothes above where Evie's knee seemed to be. He squeezed it. He said 'Thank you for listening.'

She said 'Oh that's all right.'

'Is Sophie still in New York?'

'As far as I know.'

'One goes in and out between story and reality, between what matters and what doesn't, between instincts and what might be God.'

'Now you're off again.'

'Sorry.'

He tried to remember what in his story he thought he would find if he climbed back over the wall from the garden of the school into the garden of the old man and the woman next door. It was as if that house and garden was where he had once lived and in which he had been brought up; where one had been told that one might change things by setting out with a spade and pickaxe, by pulling things up by the roots and replanting them. And this perhaps was what had been taught in the school next door, except that there they had also learnt that this didn't work. So one had to be aware of this, and watch and listen, and see what happened. Was that it? And perhaps make a bit of a joke of things. Even a bit of a fool of oneself. Was that what that chap on the Net had been doing?

So what should happen to the old school in his story? There should be a fire? There was nothing too outlandish about a fire. Someone might have left the gas on in the physics lab in the basement.

But now Evie was saying 'How do you tell the difference?'

He said 'What?'

'Between stories and reality. Between what matters and what does not.'

'I think you learn it. Make it.'

'What, reality?'

'Well, at least the difference.'

And then, because Evie seemed to be getting a hand on to some sort of lifeboat – 'What I think matters enormously is that we have been able to talk about this.'

PART TWO

12

Her parents had not seen Sophie for some time. After leaving school and during her years at university, she had used holiday periods to get temporary work at the Institute for Molecular Research; then after graduation she had been enrolled along with other selected students in a project in America that was said to be hush-hush. She had assured her parents – 'That's not because if news of it got out this would be threatening, but because the set-up would lose its air of importance.'

Adam said 'That's why a lot of government work is hush-hush.'

Evie said 'There you go again.'

Sophie said 'It's like the work of the scientists in Iran and Israel who were once upon a time trying to find a biological agent that would wipe out one racial group and not others.'

Evie said 'But that would have been important?'

Adam said 'How on earth do you think you can define scientifically a particular racial group?'

Sophie said 'I suppose its importance was if it kept them from doing any similar project that might work.'

When Sophie went to America, it was to work for an agency loosely affiliated to the United Nations. The job was to sort and classify the almost infinite amount of information that was garnered each day from communication networks all over the world. This information had to be sifted into what might or might not be considered important by people who had power. At the level at which the random mass of such information came in, it seemed practical to use clever post-graduates for the job. Sophie thought – But it is at this level that quite unimportant people might wield power!

She imagined a conversation with her parents. – For instance, what unverified rumour about the existence of weapons of mass destruction should be classified as important?

Evie would say – But every such rumour should go into the pending tray until it is verified.

Adam would say – Or until someone's oil supply is threatened.

Adam had written an article for a popular magazine in which he had said that it was in the interests of powerful democratic nations to believe that other nations were developing weapons of mass destruction in order to justify the undemocratic actions they might feel they needed to take to protect their power. This instinct was more potent than any sense of absurdity or guilt they might feel if they later learned that their suspicions had been baseless.

Evie had said – But nothing's more absurd than the useless use of tanks and bombs in war.

Adam had said – The only sure non-absurdity available to politicians would seem to be to recognise that most of their conjectures are likely to be absurd.

When Sophie arrived in New York she was taken to an address that was said to be hush-hush where selected post-graduates like herself were lodged. And perhaps they would still be being screened?

Sophie was interviewed by a man who seemed to be trying to find out not so much whether she could be trusted as what might be the criteria for such a judgement. Sophie felt he even might be wanting her to help him with this. Then would this mean that he trusted her?

A tricky one, this. Like a knot in the trunk of a tree.

When Sophie began her job, sitting in front of a computer screen and thinking – But what for goodness sake are my own criteria for this task? Should I try to believe that my judgements might be objective, or should I acknowledge that they, as with any other judgement, are a matter of personal attitude, endeavour, experience, style? Even if on such attributes might hang the question of whether or not the world will be blown up?

Oceans of flotsam from the internet wafted into her computer; debris from the ravages of famines, atrocities, wars, droughts, floods. She thought – But if one acknowledges that judgement about all this is finally up to oneself, then does there not in fact grow within one the sense that there is something helping or working through one?

– And need this be false?

She went for walks by the river; she explored art galleries. She thought – These painters, sculptors, artists – were they not discovering, uncovering, what was important, life-giving, as well as portraying it?

– And this was an ability they were experiencing not just within themselves?

She did not easily make friends with other people in the lodgings. She wondered if they had all been instructed to keep a wary eye on one another as part of the routines of this untrusting and untrustworthy world.

She did however manage to get into some relationship with a young Chinese man who was said to have spent time in Iran. She thought – It's probably difficult enough to know what's going on within a relationship with any young Chinese man, without wondering what he's been up to in Iran.

He would say things like – 'Of course Iran wants to be thought to possess a nuclear bomb. This is the only way of making it unlikely that America will use her bombs on it. But of course it doesn't want to have to be actually making a nuclear bomb, because this diverts resources from a lot of other things more useful.' Then he added – 'And anyway, Iranians are wise and civilised enough to know that who comes out a winner in such a war is a loser.'

Sophie said 'Are you a Christian?'

He said 'Why do you ask?'

'Because that's the sort of thing my father says a good Christian should say.'

'It's what any good person should know.'

She thought – There are hush-hush Christians in China?

When she wrote home to her parents she did not tell them much about her life except her visits to art galleries. She thought – They will know that this is my true hush-hush work.

When she was splashing about in the swamps of transcripts, recordings, blogs, broadcasts, intercepts, e-mails, she wondered what agency or system might conceivably make any pattern out of the rubbish. Would it not simply be what her father called chance?

– Or the capacity of those almost infinite number of monkeys who in eternity tap out the whole of Shakespeare?

She said to her Chinese friend – 'But if the Iranians are not building a bomb but want us to think they are, why do we play into their hands by saying that we think they are?'

'Because our interests are the same. To ensure domestic cohesion, we each need to feel the threat of enemies.'

'But if they know this, will that encourage them to build a bomb, or not bother to build a bomb?'

'Indeed.'

'You mean that's chance?'

'Or whatever you want to call it.'

She would go for walks with her Chinese friend along the bank of the East River north from the United Nations building. She would find herself thinking – But if conversations about practical affairs go round and round pointlessly, why don't we just go to bed together?

Her Chinese friend once said 'I used to think that the Iranians were waiting for the Western capitalist world to collapse under the weight of its contradictions.'

She said 'And what do you think now?'

'I think that they, like me, like everyone else, don't know what to think.'

She thought – So might we just collapse into bed together?

– But surely there's some way of influencing events!

They would go in their walks past a district of fashionable tower-blocks which contained the apartments of celebrities and diplomats. Small planes and helicopters flew to and fro in the permitted air-space above the river.

Then one day a plane veered off course and crashed into the side of an apartment building and exploded there. There was an immediate and general terrorist alert.

Sophie and her Chinese friend watched from a distance. Firemen unrolled equipment, and police formed lines against crowds running here and there. Sophie said 'But couldn't we make something interesting from this?'

Her Chinese friend said 'What?'

'Well, what about – The American ambassador to the UN was on his way to have an important meeting with the delegate from North Korea when he learnt that the delegate was in bed with his girlfriend. I mean the ambassador's girlfriend. I mean his spies told him that the delegate had been seen entering her apartment, so the ambassador tried to fly his light aircraft in through her window.'

'Why would that be interesting?'

'Well, it would take people's minds off just as ridiculous but more dangerous stories.'

'Why would the ambassador want to get in through her window?'

'Look, it's not supposed to make sense!'

'Perhaps because the North Korean would have got his henchmen to guard her door.'

'Exactly. It's supposed to be funny.'

'But also serious.'

'Yes.'

'That's good.'

'Thank you.'

They walked on. She thought – How much needle, or absurdity, does it take before one gets to bed?

One evening they walked to a rougher part of the town where a bridge arched across the river like cannon-fire and then exploded into traffic on the near bank. Her Chinese friend was saying 'But nothing works as intended if you try to fix it. You've got to guide it by letting things take their course.'

She said 'Guide it?'

'Yes. By knowing this is what you're doing.'

'Ah, you're a Taoist!'

'You might say so.'

'But you can't say it!'

'No.'

They had turned in towards the centre of the north end of Manhattan, which was a part of the city they had been told to avoid. There were rival ethnic groups here, and gangs on the prowl.

She thought – But we seem to have been leading each other up some very equivocal garden path.

Her Chinese friend said 'I've been warned that in this sort of area I might be taken as a North Korean, and so might be rubbed out.'

'Should we turn back?'

'I don't think so.'

They were passing the entrance to what looked like a disorderly bar or café tucked under a fly-over from the bridge. Sophie's Chinese friend suddenly turned and ducked in through the door. She thought – For God's sake, what, you're taking up a challenge? From me? You've seen something you want to avoid?

She followed him into a dark crowded room where the walls were expanding and contracting with music like the inside of a drum. The noise from the traffic outside was drowned. She thought – This is where a crime could be committed and wouldn't be recorded.

She followed him to the counter of the bar, and on their way the music suddenly stopped and it was as if their entrance might have caused this. There had been people in the centre of the room dancing, writhing with their arms up like snakes in a pit; now they stopped with their heads on one another's shoulders or turned towards Sophie and her friend. Sophie thought – You mean, we didn't choose to come here? You're letting things take their course? All right, let them.

At the counter there were older men with their hats or caps on and their elbows on the counter. They had had their backs to the dancers; now, without the music, they turned and watched Sophie and her Chinese friend approaching. They did not make way for them at the counter, so Sophie's friend spoke over their heads – 'Two beers please.' Sophie, standing behind him, said 'I'd like a small one.' A man at the counter said in an affected voice 'She'd like a small one!' and made a noise like someone sucking. Sophie thought – I could have meant it as a joke? Then – Or they want to think my friend is North Korean? She might explain – North Koreans are only trying to get a bomb in order to stop you people wanting to bomb them flat. But what a hope.

She looked round at the men at the counter and saw them as if they were people acting in a film: how do fights start in a bar like this in a film? Someone nudges someone, someone is insulted, someone draws a gun – or drops a bomb. But people wait for someone to make the first move. She could see her Chinese friend's face in the mirror behind the bar; he was looking down at the counter absorbed and removed, as if he were waiting for something to happen – although, all right, he need not know what it might be. She thought – He is acting? Not acting? Acting not acting? I helped to get him here, all right, but it was his action to come in. The man behind the bar was doing nothing to get him his drinks. She thought – But in films, isn't it traditional that after a fight a man and a woman get to go to bed together?

A man at the counter seemed to have been nudged. He said 'Watch what you're doing' or 'Watcha watta doin' or 'Kosher blogger blew in.' But the music had started again.

A man came up behind Sophie and put his arms round her. Her Chinese friend had his back to her at the bar. She tried to convey to him – Now stay like that! Don't move! I can handle this! But after a moment he turned and faced her, and the music was too loud for anything to be heard. Several people started laughing. She thought

– But I have no idea what to do! So do you mean, that makes it all right then? The man holding her lifted her as if she were a sack. Her Chinese friend was looking over her shoulder towards the door.

Two large Chinese-looking men had come in – or this was what Sophie saw in the mirror at the back of the bar. The two men seemed to be taking stock of the room and in particular herself and her Chinese friend who was facing them. But because her view was in reflection, might it be an illusion? Or could it have been these two men that her friend had spotted in the street? They were minders put on by their agency to follow them? Or perhaps her Chinese friend was in fact a North Korean suspect under surveillance, so might he now make a sudden dash for the door and the two men would seize him and take him outside and beat him up; or would they have rescued him and her from their absurd predicament? What would make the best film story?

Anyway now the man who had lifted her up was dumping her and letting her go. And her friend was raising a hand briefly as if to acknowledge the two men by the door. Then he took her by the arm and turned her and they moved towards the door. No one tried to stop them. The two Chinese-looking men made way for them.

When they were out in the street and no one had followed them, Sophie thought – Perhaps they were after all just two men dropping in for a drink.

However – Whatever has happened or not happened, it doesn't seem to have made it easier to go to bed.

13

Adam sat in front of his computer and tried to remember the scenes he had been writing at the beginning of his story – about God and the Garden of Eden and the necessity for children to get out; and God realising that when humans were out of the Garden they would tend to make Him seem to have done something unpleasant, in order to be able to excuse what they would now see as their own tendency to unpleasantness. But to leave things like that was no good, because God's job was surely to help humans to use their freedom to understand what life out of the Garden could be like if they saw both themselves and Him truly as (to say the least) not unpleasant.

And so now where was he, Adam, in the story of how a human or humans might manage this? To learn, that is, how a partnership between God and humans might be not only pleasant but necessary?

Or vice versa? Which made the best sense.

Was this why he had brought in Sophie's Chinese friend and thus Taoism – Tao being awareness of the conjunction of God without and God within, thus putting humans into relationship with forces that govern nature and the universe –

– But so long as this was not talked about?

Did any of this make sense?

And so on.

Evie, thank goodness, now came in with a cup of tea. He said 'I'm in a state of self-satisfied doubt.'

Evie said 'Here's your tea.'

He said 'It's all right if one knows it's confusion. The world goes on its way in confusion. Human nature is confusion. What is not confusion is to be aware of this.'

'Drink it before it gets cold.'

'I've come to a point where, if it's to be contemporary, God help it, I've got to say a bit more about sex. But now I don't know if it's relevant.'

'Why not?'

'Sex is like the big bang – necessary for creation. Lots of little bits and pieces whizzing about and forming galaxies. Then run-of-the-mill gravity takes over.'

'What's run-of-the-mill gravity?'

'The birds and the bees. Bringing up children. Making you comfy, as they say in massage parlours.'

'I don't want to hear about massage parlours.'

'But that's what most sex is after the first big bang. Shooting or shifting one's load, as they say. With the exception of you and me, of course, who go on banging away happily.'

Adam pushed back his chair. He could not decide whether to turn off his computer or to let it lapse into its own hibernation. This was the sort of thing that had to take its own course? Evie looked over his shoulder at what he had written. She said 'Is this about Sophie in New York?'

'Yes.'

'What on earth is she doing?'

'I wanted to get her hooked up with a Muslim Sufi, but she's got herself tied in with a Chinaman instead.'

'Why?'

'I don't know. I suppose because Muslims have become identified with not making sense. I mean, they may have got their God right – he appears both merciful and vindictive, ruthless and compassionate. But they don't seem to have got it all together, to handle it.'

'I thought you approved of Sufis.'

'Yes I do. But they seem more concerned with keeping their heads down rather than stopping ordinary Muslims blowing themselves and others up.'

'I suppose ordinary Muslims want to go straight to heaven.'

'Yes, and that's not a Tao thing. Aren't you clever!'

'Didn't you say somewhere you've got a brilliant wife?'

'Yes I do!'

'I suppose what you really mean is aren't you clever!'

'Yes. No. What?'

The screen of his computer suddenly went blank. This always made him jump. One day the universe might suddenly go blank – God having pushed either the wrong or the right button.

Evie said 'Well I'll leave you to it.'

Sophie and her Chinese friend were walking through New York's Central Park. It was now late at night, and they were wondering if the park might officially be closed because it seemed so deserted. Or it might be just that people were afraid of muggers? On the road that wound through the park there were the lights of traffic, but even these seemed like the lanterns of police looking for clues to a murder.

Sophie's Chinese friend was saying – 'There's a lot of evidence that when sex is a free-for-all it explodes or implodes, goes into sadism and masochism or whatever. But if it's too restricted by rules and conventions then it goes into boredom and frustration – I suppose into bombs in cars or strapped round one's middle.'

Sophie said 'So what's the answer?'

'No answer. One becomes aware of being used to one's predicament.'

'And then?'

'Things happen.'

'Doubtless.'

'Perhaps one thing rather than another.'

She thought – Here I am walking with a man I hardly know through Central Park at night, and we're brave enough to do this but apparently too sophisticated or hooked on waffle to know how to get to bed.

She said 'My father says pornography is nowadays about women suspending men by their balls from the ceiling.'

'Do you watch pornography?'

'No.'

'What is your fantasy?'

Sophie thought – Well your fantasy seems to be that we can't hop into bed because this would have to fit in with what you and my father would call the forces of the universe. Or some such salmagundi.

She said 'One of my fantasies is that I am a servant-girl and although I don't think I've done anything wrong, I have accepted that I may have to be punished. This is because it would be some sort of liberation from obligation, from super-ego, like getting out of the Garden of Eden.'

'You mean punished sexually?'

'I suppose so. Or ethically.' She wondered – Am I implying these are the same thing?

He said – 'You mean, humans may like to have something to repent about, because then it means that they will have been able to sin?'

She thought – Good heavens, is that what my father means?

She said 'Is that the right way round? But it seems part of nature. To want to get things both ways.'

'Not logical.'

'Oh no!'

'And liable to go wrong?'

'Naturally.'

She thought – Perhaps we really get on too well together. And this is to do with love, not sex.

He said 'You like playing games?'

She thought – Oh Lord, come and rescue me!

She said 'I'm not sure.'

'One is apt to get the giggles.'

She thought – What's wrong with giggles?

Or – He really is very clever!

She said 'But I see one can't talk about it.'

'One has to wait for the right moment. For fantasy and reality to be combined.'

She thought – But he really can be very pompous.

Then it seemed that there might be footsteps coming up behind them, for he turned suddenly and span on one leg and did one of those balletic kicks that one sees in Japanese movies (or were they Chinese?) that she always thought so absurd. His kick (as usual) did not seem to connect with anything. Was it always just play-acting? Then he crouched, and pulled her down at the side of the path beside him. She thought – Oh well, I see, we might at least now have a fumble. Or were there really muggers? Even – Why not those two Chinese-looking men who had after all been coming after us? He held her tightly, with his head down against her as if he were praying. And there were now shadows wafting around them as if in a wind.

After a time they stood up and walked on. She thought – All right, I am somewhat humbled, as well as presumptuous and arrogant.

He said 'We should get into some streets.'

'Yes.'

'And then we might find a hotel.'

'That would be pleasant.'

The old man who had been both the history master and the head-master of the school, and the woman who was said to be both his mistress and the science mistress, came to peer through a gap in the garden wall which had been made by the fire-fighters so they could direct their hoses at the blaze which had recently ravaged the school. It was said that a naked flame had been left on in the science laboratory in the basement. The effects of the fire, combined with the efforts of the fire-brigade to deal with it, had left the building looking not so different from outside but gutted and hollow within. The old man and the mistress had found an angle at the gap in the wall from which they could see right through from one side of the school to daylight on the other. The old man said 'History's gone, Literature's gone, Languages have gone. They were pretty well buggered anyway. I can't remember where Social Studies and Media Studies were. Were they anywhere? I suppose Science is still in the basement.'

The woman said 'We were doing most of the work outside anyway.'

'I never saw the point of that story about men with skull caps and black beards. Haven't there always been men with skull caps and black beards?'

'I liked the one about the child with the model aeroplane stuffed with explosives.'

'And the pilot was killed?'

'So they say.'

'That was a joke?'

'Presumably the child survived.'

The old man and the woman moved back into the house. He said 'Who was that chap who seemed to think he knew all about it? Did he get the girls out in time?'

'He's under suspicion.'

'He wasn't a teacher?'

'Yes, but he wanted to alter the curriculum.'

'That sounds more like a child.'

'Well it wasn't him who wanted to blow the place up.'

The old man and the woman entered the conservatory. While he had been in the garden the old man had walked with a stick. Now he slumped into his wheel chair, and because he hadn't got the brakes on he shot backwards.

He said 'I thought that science was the one thing that couldn't change.'

'No that's old-fashioned.'

'Then how did he want to alter things?'

'I think he wanted there to be a story.'

'Why?'

'Then we could make up our own minds.'

'He seemed to think we were all a story.'

'Yes, about how things might change.'

The old man practised spinning himself round in his chair. Then he said 'I thought science was the one thing that couldn't change.'

She said 'No, that's old-fashioned.'

'Have we said this before?'

'Yes.'

'Have I got Alzheimer's?'

'I don't know.'

'Then how do things change?'

'By your being conscious of them.'

'Then they change?'

'Perhaps.'

The old man span in his chair. He said 'That's gobbledegook.'

'Perhaps.'

'Are people beginning to think like that?'

'A few.'

'Have I got Alzheimer's?'

'I don't know.'

'And it's by being conscious of most things being gobbledegook that things can change?'

'Yes.'

'That's gobbledegook.' He span in his chair again. Then he said 'So what's changed?'

'I don't know.'

'Have I got Alzheimer's?'

'Perhaps.'

'But I wouldn't know if I had, would I?'

'Wouldn't you?'

'So what's changed?'

Evie was looking at the pages that Adam's computer had printed and were lying on his desk. She was thinking – All right, you're getting to the sex; will it be the big bang or the birds and the bees?

Adam came into the room. He was wearing a track-suit and trainers. He said 'There are crowds in the streets demanding that the underground should be reopened, and other crowds demanding that it should remain permanently closed.'

Evie said 'Were there or weren't there muggers in the park.'

He said 'What?' Then he saw the pages on the desk that Evie had been reading. He said 'I haven't printed out the latest bit yet.'

Evie said 'Either things are or aren't.'

'No, that's old-fashioned. My mistress says things have changed. They can now both be and not be at the same time.'

'Your mistress?'

'The science mistress. I've been out in the park. I wanted to see how easy it would be to spin in a wheelchair.'

'But he isn't in a wheelchair.'

'Who?'

'Your Chinaman.'

'It isn't my Chinaman. It's my history master. I found an old man in a wheelchair. I asked him if I could try it.'

'Try what?'

'Spinning round and round like they do in the Olympics. Research.'

'You're not making sense.'

'No. You haven't got there yet.'

Adam sat in front of his computer. He turned it on. He thought – So it's not easy, no, to spin round and round in a wheelchair.

Evie said 'Have you heard from Sophie?'

He said 'I thought she'd met this Chinese man in New York.'

'But something either is a story or isn't.'

'No, that's what's old-fashioned.' Then – 'I thought we'd been through all this.' He wondered – Is it me who's got Alzheimer's?

'Through what?'

'We all write our stories. Are part of other people's stories.' Then – 'Look, I'm trying to write it!'

'All right! I just came up to talk about Sophie.'

'Talk about what?'

'I'm worried. I haven't heard from her.'

'Can't you get her on her mobile?'

'She's not answering.'

'Perhaps she's with her Chinese man.'

'What's that supposed to mean?'

'Ah! That's the question! Yes!' Adam stared at his computer, where text was coming up on the screen.

Evie said 'Oh really!' and left the room.

When Sophie and her Chinese friend had found a room in a hotel it was indeed as if they had been washed up on a strange shore where something new might grow. But should they not first make, or have made, some shelter, a home? She thought – To establish peace, we need to have children. But haven't we been saying that sex is a form of war?

She sat on the edge of the bed with her hands clenched on her knees. She said 'I'd like to give birth to a new world.'

He said 'It might be done.'

'Can we wait?'

'Of course.'

She thought – I might sit here like a painting in one of those caves for thousands of years and then if the tomb or womb were opened I would disappear.

– The world is evil. The world is good. How can these be made to be experienced as one?

Adam pushed himself back from his computer. He thought – This is crazy, I have no idea where I am going.

– I have to be accepting that that is the point?

Evie seemed to have left the house. Perhaps she was hoping to find a more amenable lover. With luck she would not go under a bus.

In his story Eve had got bored in the Garden? So God had said – All right, come and sit on my knee?

God knows what he is doing. One has to see him as a bit of a chancer, in order for life to be bearable. Not a disciplinarian, but a gambler. Not explicable, but bearable.

On the news that morning there had been pictures of bits of bombed children with their limbs indistinguishable from rubble.

Sophie sat on the edge of the bed with her hands clenched on her knees. She said 'One would have to be able to see the whole of life all at once for it to be bearable.'

Her friend said 'All right, why not?'

'Because it's not possible.'

She remembered an image of a mother, any mother, being taken down to a basement to identify bits of her child.

Her friend came and put an arm round her. He said 'Don't worry, we needn't do anything.'

She thought – I'm so sorry. But then, how does life go on?

He helped to lie her down on the bed so that she was on her back staring at the ceiling. He looked down on her as if from a great height. He thought – Why are there so few female Buddhas, Bodhisattvas, sitting up cross-leg and looking smug? Because they hope not to escape from an old world, but to give birth to a new one?

He climbed over her taking care not to touch her, and lay on his back on her far side. He stared at the ceiling. He thought perhaps he might project a picture on to the ceiling which she would be able to see.

He was a small child in the village in which he had been born and brought up. His family had been taken away at the time of the revolution. He was sitting on the ground alone in the square in which there had been the temple which was the glory of the village. It had elaborate decoration and mosaics which were now smashed and scattered in jagged pieces around the square. On an outer wall there had been a huge Tree of Life in which birds were depicted as dwelling. The tree had been hacked at but had not fallen; the bits of glass and mosaic were now like seeds around the square. The birds might have managed to fly? They might return to eat the seeds and then new trees might grow from their droppings.

Sophie lay beside him. She was so beautiful! They did not need the explosion of sex. They might walk barefoot, hand in hand, over glass and mosaic like light. Their feet might bleed; but this might help things to grow.

Adam's fingers fluttered above the keys of his computer. They were like birds. How could he bring them to land? He would just finish the sentence he was writing, then he should go and lie down.

14

Evie had become irritated with Adam, but then when she was out of his room and going down the stairs she was thinking – But I should stop resenting his computer. I should be out and about seeing what he is trying to get Sophie and her Chinese man to do, or what he is trying to show. But what on earth is this: the need to risk something? To go into some area of danger? With the idea that good and evil are interwoven – in life, in God? Well all right, what is the point of the crucifixion if it is not to do with salvation. Gobbledegook! But should one not try and see?

In her volatile mood she thought she might go to a rough part of the town as Sophie and her Chinese man had done – and risk being mugged, beaten up, raped? This did not make sense! But then why was such a carry-on becoming so popular at weekends: because there were no more authorised tortures, beheadings, disembowelments, at least in so-called civilised countries. And so people had to go to some lengths to get their reactive spiritual thrills. Was this what Adam was getting at? Getting oneself blown up – well this was held by some to be a theological thing to do, to be sure; not only to get oneself to heaven but to get the world sorted. But she, Evie, was too old for this! What sort of story, written on pulped skin, could be made from her?

She did not, thank God, care much about sex any more. Though it was good of Adam to have said that they still had occasionally what might be called a big bang. And what did she really care about sorting out the world; unless it was perhaps theologically?

But there was some impulse, itch, pushing her.

She waited until it was evident that Adam had settled down again with his computer, then she went out into the street. Here people seemed to be going about their business quietly and not quite blindly. Even with bits of machinery stuck to their ears, they seemed to be looking inwardly if not outwardly.

She had sometimes thought it would be interesting to go to a sleazy part of the town about which one read stories in the papers about drugs and sex and young girls vomiting in the gutter. And Evie knew nothing of this, but believed it, because it fitted in with what she had gathered about human nature and religion. So why did one not go to look: because one feared one might find something unexpected? Sophie had suggested a lot of it was exaggerated – emphasised by an older generation to put blame for their failings on a new. Well Sophie would, wouldn't she? And Adam blathered on about atonement. And this was all Evie knew about not knowing about it.

But if she got into trouble there, Adam would not know how to find her?

She and Adam had watched a television film the previous night – a murder mystery in which all the suspects had lied and thus had made things worse for themselves. But like this the interest had been drawn out over two hours; and without lies how on earth would the actors and audience have passed the time? If they'd set out to tell the truth at the beginning, they'd have had soon to move on to something other than murder: and then what of the ratings?

Adam had said – What differentiates humans from animals is lies. This may be done for self-preservation, but it also gives them the technique and space to try to get things sorted. Then – But they should surely remember what they're up to.

Evie went to the underground, which showed no signs of having been bombed or abandoned. She thought – We tunnel into tombs like the Pyramids. Do suicide bombers think they are doing us a favour?

But what an odd story that was of Sophie telling her Chinese man her fantasy about the need to be punished for liberation!

Or that was Adam's imagination?

Evie emerged from the underground in a different part of the town where there were no high-rise buildings and shops seemed to have had their tops knocked off as Sophie's old school had done. Black and Chinese-looking men moved as if wandering away from music; women in black *hijabs* or *niqabs* (what was the word?) glided on their hobby-horses like ghosts. Evie stumbled along as if following on foot an illegal hunt. She thought – I may be too old to be molested, but not to be beaten up or robbed.

Muffled music arose from a narrow basement area. She did not know what sort of music it might be; things nowadays had to have a name. The music cartwheeled along without seeming to need to reach a climax. She remembered Adam's story about the man having his balls torn off, and the joke about whether in these circumstances he could have reached his desired climax.

She had paused by the railings above the basement area. She thought – No one will ask me in, both because I am too old, and because it will not help me to try to explain the serious nature of my research. – Gentlemen, is everything for the best in even the worst of all possible worlds because it makes no sense to say how it could not be?

And I can't exactly ask to be taken down to the cellar.

An old man who seemed to be drunk came up and he held out his hand. She took his hand and shook it; then realised he must have been asking for money. She opened the front flaps of her coat as if to indicate that she had not got any money. Then she saw that this might give a wrong impression too.

The old man nodded, and took her by the arm.

She thought – Well either I go through with this or I don't.

He led her to a door at street level that was above the basement from which the music came. She thought – But if I am to play my part in the redemption of myself or the world, I really do need a drink first. She might explain to whatever company there happened to be in the basement – Gentlemen, I will do what I can by suffering to absolve you from your sins, but I really must get sloshed.

The door from the street was opened by a tall, rather beautiful black man. The old man who was still holding her spoke to him in a language that she did not understand.

She thought – If he is trying to sell me, might I not charge a commission? Then I could buy my own drink.

– But of course, I am only pretending not to have money. So what is happening now, one way or another, is this the outcome of a desire for truth, or a lie?

The black man stood back from the door and they went through. She thought – I can see how there can be misunderstandings. Or – I may be a witch, watch it.

The black man led the way down some stairs to the basement where there was a door from behind which the music was coming. The noise was very loud – perhaps to replace, or to drown, the screams of people being tortured. But there must be something jolly about all this, or how could it be so popular? The black man was indicating that the old man should not come any further: the old man let go of her and held out his hand. Evie thought – And a tip for the victim, please, so I can buy my own drink without exposure as a liar.

The black man took a small packet from his pocket and handed it to the old man. The old man took it and went back up the stairs. Evie thought – Hey, I'd like some of that! Please.

When the door into the basement room was opened, the noise that emerged was like the heat of an oven. Dancers were jerking with their arms up as if begging for an escape through the roof; perhaps for hands to come down from heaven to help them. Evie thought – Does one really have to go through something like this to become joined with God if not in heaven then of course even better on earth? Or were the dancers just trying to separate some unwanted bits of their bodies from others, as if with bombs? The walls of the room expanded and contracted like the pulse of heartbeats in a womb. The people were all black or brown so that it was mainly their energy that stood out in the darkness. Evie stood by the rather beautiful black man who had let her in and held her hand out as the old man had done. She thought – If I am doped, drugged, I will have made myself amenable. The dancers had not seemed to notice her when she came in; now they began to throw glances at her like hot embers. She thought – But if I am in a different world, will Adam or Sophie indeed ever find me?

Her black friend was handing her a drooping tube of paper like a damp cigarette. She thought – But first I must sit before I fall. Some women were feeling the material of her coat; she wanted to say – All right, you can have it, but you must first help me take it off. They did this; then held it up as if it were the skin of an animal. She had quickly taken a few puffs of her joint or whatever you called it; she was now sitting on a mattress on the floor at a lower level to that of the rather beautiful black man who had his hands on her shoulders. She thought she might say – Carry me along, taddy, like you done through the toy fair. Where did this come from: surely not one of Jesus's last words from the cross? She could say to Adam – The reason why there is not more pornography about men torturing women is because it is surely in everyone's interests for women to stay beautiful? And what had been happening to her so far had not been unpleasant. The dope in fact was helping her to begin to feel that she might be about to dip her toe into one of the supreme oceanic moments in the universe.

She could tell herself – Don't make me laugh! But wasn't St. Lawrence supposed to have laughed with those men setting him up on his grid-iron?

What was it that Sophie had said in Adam's story? – I want to give birth to a new world?

15

An Israeli tank-commander called Simeon protruded from the waist above the turret of his tank. He was looking across the border into Lebanon which, he had been taught as a child, was part of the land of Israel that had been promised by God to Abraham, and this promise had been confirmed to Moses and Joshua and goodness knows who else. Simeon had looked up this story in the Torah the other day because the extent of the promised territory had seemed so vast that he had wondered if it might have been a bit of modern political propaganda. So he had dug out exactly what had been said to Moses in the book of Deuteronomy – 'Go to the mount of the Amorites, and unto all the places nigh thereunto in the plain, and in the hills, and in the vale, and in the south, and by the seaside; and to the land of the Canaanites, and unto Lebanon, unto the great river, the river Euphrates.' So there it was. All right. But were the Israelis now taking note that they had been instructed to occupy the area all the way from Egypt to the Euphrates? And so were they supposed to be responsible even for sorting out Baghdad?

Much of the previous day Israeli bombers had been flying over Simeon's head with the intention, it seemed, of bombing the land of the Canaanites (was it?) flat. But could this be quite what God and Moses had had in mind? The main effect of the bombing, so far as Simeon could see, was to make it impossible for his tanks to advance over the jagged piles of rubble, and to provide material for the Amorites (might they be?) to build impregnable dugouts and defence-works. Surely God's advice to the Israelites would be somewhat different in modern political and military conditions.

And anyway, was there not a belief amongst some Israelis that God had rescinded his promise to Abraham and Moses at the time when the Romans had lost patience with the Israelites in the so-called first century AD, and had turned them out of their country and destroyed their temple. God had allowed this, so the theory went, because the Israelites had been so fractious and incompetent in running the country that God had given them, that God had decided that from now on they should be scattered and should remain so, and should now influence the world just by the example of their probity and obedience to his laws. This should continue till the coming of the promised Messiah – after which, who knows: the end of the world? Simeon had been drawn to this way of seeing things because in his experience the exercise of worldly power did indeed lead to corruption.

It had also struck him that the scattering of the Jews and the withdrawal of God's promise of worldly power had happened almost coincidentally with the life and death of Jesus and the origins of Christianity. Jesus, a Jew, had eschewed worldly power, and indeed had said that his mission was to all nations. It was not clear whether Jesus had felt himself to be the promised Messiah; but Simeon had for some time thought it odd that Israeli authorities, both religious and secular, seemed to pay no attention whatever to these coincidences.

When dawn broke the day after the most savage bombing yet of southern Lebanon, Simeon was watching through binoculars for any signs of life from the ruins of the nearest village across the border. He was wondering – Well, what happens now if humans still seem to be getting the use of power so wrong: doesn't God do anything except give and take back promises? No wonder our theologians seem to have given up the ghost of serious inquiry; to have taken refuge behind skull caps and beards.

Through his binoculars he saw a solitary small figure emerge from the rubble across the border. It was impossible to tell at first if it was an old person who had been wounded, or a child. It made its way slowly round and over the terrain of desolation till it came to the stretch of open ground between it and the fence which marked the border between Israel and Lebanon, across which Simeon's tanks faced. The figure moved hesitantly, as if exhausted, or perhaps unused to walking, but still determined. It was dressed in what appeared to be rags or possibly a gathered-up bed-sheet. It was heading towards the tanks. Simeon had his instructions about persons trying to cross the border who might be potential suicide bombers – or rather not instructions, because these could not exactly be spelt out – but the understanding was there: 'Shoot first and ask questions later. Do not take risks, and you will be protected if there are troublesome consequences later.' It was known from traumatic experience that a tank could instantly be turned into a death-oven by a bomber.

The figure of a child, or someone wounded, had reached the fence. When it bent to look or to climb between the wires Simeon saw its face for the first time. It was indeed the face of a child, yes; but what a strange child! Half smiling, in a knowing but almost self-effacing way. So what should he, Simeon, do? He had had the child, or whatever it was, covered with his automatic weapon all the way to the fence from where it had emerged from the rubble. But now it was climbing through and then coming on steadily. It was heading to pass close to, or through, his line of tanks. Simeon was the officer in charge; he was on watch; the others would probably be sleeping. There was a bit of poetry he had learned at school that was trying to force its way into his head. He felt now that he should keep his gun out of sight while he watched the figure intently. The child passed close to his tank; it remained slightly crouched, not looking to right or left, but seeming to be aware of him. The lines of poetry broke through into his head; they were about a 'rough beast, its hour come round at last,' that 'slouches towards Bethlehem to be born.' Yes, that was it. And the child did seem to be smiling. And whatever it was up to, the message it carried would surely be different from that delivered to Abraham and Moses?

The Old Man and Lilith were peering over the edge of their precipice trying to see what was happening on the plains below. The Old Man had the latest hi-tech telescope which made use of the speed of light as infinity. He said, as he so often did, 'What the devil are they up to?' Lilith said 'It's partly your responsibility. You've got such a poor grasp of geography.'

'I have to leave some things to interpretation. I'm not good at geography. Who are the Canaanites? Anyway, I was singing a song.'

'What song?'

'That one that goes on and on about ten green bottles hanging on the wall. And if one green bottle should accidentally fall – '

'And what's that got to do with Moses and Joshua?'

The Old Man sang – 'And if one green King of Canaan should accidentally fall – ' He laughed.

'Oh really!'

The Old Man looked gratified. He liked an excuse to sing. He said 'No one takes the words of anyone else's songs literally. And anyway, it's you who are supposed to be keeping an eye on them.'

'You're always hogging the telescope.'

'It's amazing technology. Or is it theology? If everything is relative, then light in relation to itself is instantaneous, and you can see all bits and pieces all at once and for ever all the way to the Red Sea.'

'It's not the Red Sea now, it's the Dead Sea, or the Med.'

'Oh well what's the difference?'

'They'll be expecting you to part the waters for them soon.'

'Doesn't that now mean giving birth?'

'Well we've agreed, haven't we, that nowadays it's to do with the individual?'

It had been understood that Sophia should keep an eye on Evie, but nowadays Sophia was so taken up with experiments about what, in an age of darkness, should be the function of light, that she had asked Lilith to stand in for her as in the old days. It had been gathered that Evie was feeling a bit left out because of the time Adam spent with his computer; also perhaps because of what she felt was his interest in Sophie's young friends whom he had met at her school. And were they not all of them – Adam and Sophie and the girls and other characters in his story – spending too much time in speculation about 'reality': what was within the mind and what was outside it; what was a story made up by humans and what was not? Should they not rather just be getting on with it?

Also Evie had apparently begun to be aggrieved that it was men who claimed to be in touch with a power of redemption through sacrifice and suffering, while women remained out of such things at best as encouragers and observers. (Evie had protested – What about childbirth!) So Evie had taken herself off (so the information went) to a rough part of the town (though had not such an idea first appeared in a story by Adam about Sophie and her Chinaman?) to see about getting in touch with some would-be 'reality.' (And was it not significant that there now seemed to be so little differentiation between Sophia and Sophie – the divine and the human – that – that – where were we? One had better get on with one's story.)

Evie had managed to get herself into some danger in a rough part of the town, though it was doubtful that she was feeling Christ-like. During the night in which she had been held captive things had developed to such a pitch, got so out of control (at least this was what she thought she remembered) – what with pot, hash, dirt, smack, and something that the rather beautiful black man referred to as his green-eyed goddess – that those who might previously have felt themselves underprivileged and who now had in their power someone who in other circumstances they might have felt privileged and so on whom they would have been glad to take their envy and resentment, now, or then (where were we? oh yes) now and then they came to find, as a result of their victim's compliance, that they were feeling quite tender towards her; and it seemed that she must be aware of the same sort of feeling too. But then the next morning – after the kind of things that had happened the night before – the question must have occurred to them all – how could her captors possibly now just let Evie go; surely she would be bound to go straight to the police and tell them her story and show them evidence of her brutal treatment. So it struck them all, including Evie, that the only practical way to prevent this would be for them to kill her.

Thus when morning came and Evie woke from strange dreams about little bits of saints preserved in glass cases in cathedrals (was that it?) – woke to find herself on the filthy mattress on the floor on which, as far as she could remember, she had been more than once raped during the night – she found her captors standing over her but now, it seemed, in a more distraught if not straightforwardly threatening frame of mind than before, because they now looked totally humourless whereas before there had been (she was surely right about this?) some jokes and laughter. In fact they looked guilty; and she herself even felt disorientated enough not to mind all that much if they were thinking of killing her. But then in her mind, through her aches and pains, she heard herself saying both to herself and to them – as if the words had been put there – I've never heard such rubbish in all my life!

But she imagined it might be difficult to put this across to them.

She sat up and said 'Look, I can't very well remember everything that happened last night, but I suspect that I was not only raped but gang-banged and buggered. I know it's a hopelessly unacceptable thing to say, but surely something like this must have been what I was looking for. Or why should I have come to his hideous part of the town? Men are always going off on expeditions to risk getting wounded or killed, and in some mysterious way they believe that in suffering like this they are doing something noble in the scheme of things. And women have encouraged them; even if, goodness knows, mainly in order to be rid of them. But now that we know something about all this, for goodness' sake, this nonsense has to stop. It's becoming too dangerous. I just wanted to see what it was like, that's all. But if you kill me now, it will just go on for ever.'

The young men who had come into the cellar as if to consider what to do about Evie looked uneasy, as men do when they find themselves in the presence of a woman giving birth to an unusual idea or a baby.

She went on – 'Look, I'd been in a state of distress because my husband got some story from pornography, or he dreams up stories about his daughter's young friends. And he says that pornography is mainly about men being maltreated by women, which it seems they can't get enough of, because they still seem to drift off to war. So I thought I'd look into this peculiar situation: what on earth is the satisfaction in pain and humiliation? Does it really offer meaning? Well? If it is offered and accepted without disaster, that is, can it really help the continuance of life, and divert one from taking out one's ruinous frustrations and furies upon others? Or at least the recognition of this. Or is this gobbledegook? Well, we'll see, won't we.'

The young men seemed to show no sings of understanding or reacting to what she was saying whatsoever.

Evie went on – 'I'm sure you yourselves feel the lack of an acceptable alternative experience, or why are you so often so violently and miserably unpleasant? Although I must say in my somewhat stoned recollection of last night a lot of it seemed to be quite jolly. But didn't you once used to stone women literally? And did that give you any sense of purgation? Do you know the word? It refers to purification, release, relief; though not perhaps without a few side effects I suppose like masturbation. Or would you rather revenge and brutality just went on for ever? Well, all I can say is, my ordeal at your hands was certainly at times painful: purgation, like giving birth, for some reason has to be painful. But the point is, what is the outcome of all this? And it seems to me, from what I have learnt of you, that you have the potentiality of being quite decent and caring.'

Evie thought – If I go on like this, they will surely kill me.

She went on – 'So what I want to say is, I am quite grateful to you. I am quite glad to have been given a fairly extensive experience of drugs, of which previously I knew nothing. And of course the drugs alleviated the pain – I suppose especially of the buggery, if that occurred, which I expect it did. And oh yes, I was even grateful for that, because it seemed a not unnatural way of not risking pregnancy. That was thoughtful of you, if you thought of it, don't you think? Ha ha, that was a joke. Oh yes, and one thing more. I've left a note on the table thanking you for your hospitality, so this should be sufficient evidence to ensure that no charges will be brought against you. So I trust you no longer think it will be necessary to kill me.'

She stood, and with some awkwardness made her way to the door. No one tried to stop her. As she passed the tall black man who had let her in the day before, she stumbled for a moment, as if in pain, and put her hand on his arm. Then she laughed.

When she was going up the stairs she said as if to herself – So was that all right, was it, old God, old Sophia, old Lilith? I lost it a bit at the end. But thank you for being with me!

And then – But in fact, I was so doped, did anything much happen at all? I can think what I like? This must be the point of dope, isn't it?

When she got home, Adam said 'Where have you been? I've been frantic!'

She thought – I don't suppose you have.

He was sitting at his computer. She kissed the top of his head.

She said 'So you bloody well should be!'

16

When Sophie awoke from a short sleep she thought at first that her Chinese friend must have gone because he was not on the bed beside her and he did not seem to have touched her. Then she saw him sitting in a chair by the window and looking out onto a blank wall across the central well of the hotel building. She thought – He is being possessed by a memory of something that still might change him.

She left the bed and moved to sit beside him. There was no other chair in the room, so she sat on the floor. From here she could see through the window to a place higher up on the facing wall than that at which he seemed to be looking. She tried to see what he might be seeing.

He said 'I'm sorry I am of no use to you.'

She said 'Why do you say that? You are.'

'Where I come from there were such terrible things done, such pleasure in destruction. It was called purification.'

'And it was not?'

'Could it have been?'

She did not know what to say.

He said 'They wanted to get rid of the past. All of it. The beautiful things above all, because they were what kept people tied to the past.'

'But you have memories?'

'Yes.'

She put her hand on his knee and rested her head against it.

He said 'We knew about torture. We knew that it made the people doing it happy.'

'But not you.'

'No. But what did I do about it.'

She tried again to think of something to say. She pressed her head against his knee.

He said 'There were people who died and people who wanted to die but were not allowed to. And for the people doing this, it was this power that seemed to make life worth living.'

She thought – Why does there not seem to be anything to say?

She said 'What were the women doing?'

'They seemed no different. I don't remember anyone doing anything unusual. How could they, when what was happening did not seem to be unusual?'

She thought she might say – But now, this is unusual.

He said 'There was a temple, a famous temple, with an outside wall on which there was a huge mosaic of the Tree of Life. They attacked this with axes, as if it were a tree. So they must have felt it was real. But this tree was made of bits of stone and glass so it was difficult to bring down: it had with such pains been constructed. And when it would not come down people tore at it with their fingers, which bled. So they called for explosives, which blew the tree to bits, and glass and stone were strewn all over the square like atoms and molecules. And people who had known the tree came to walk barefoot in the square so that their feet bled. This seemed to be all they could do.'

Sophie said 'You remember that.'

'Yes.'

'And I seem to remember it. You must have told me. It is a beautiful story.'

They remained looking across the hollow centre of the hotel building.

He said 'I am now looking at that blank wall across the courtyard. I am thinking how extraordinary it is that one brick should stay on top of another.'

She said 'Yes isn't it.'

'You do see that?'

'Yes.' Then after a time – 'It's odd, I never think of you as if you had a name.'

He said 'My name is Linn.'

'Yes I know.'

After a time he said 'Perhaps people and things are really bits and pieces until they are part of a creation.'

She thought – Perhaps we did make love.

Or – Might there be other ways of becoming pregnant?

Adam had fallen asleep in front of his computer. He awoke with a bang. His head seemed to have fallen on the keyboard. He thought – Like that tree coming down in the square. But the birds had flown?

And that's how one says what can't be said?

He brought his last page back onto the screen. He thought – Oh love, love, what is the making of love –

– One's bleeding feet?

– The bricks in the wall of a courtyard?

– A carry-on in a basement?

Or the existence of children.

He thought he should go down and find Evie. He was doing this more frequently now. What on earth in fact had Evie been up to the other night? She had a lover? What difference would that make? Should he shout and smash the furniture and bring the house down –

– Like a religious fanatic –

– Like a suicide bomber –

But the birds would have flown.

He found Evie lying on the bed on top of the bedclothes with her hands behind her head. She was staring at the ceiling as if she might be seeing some illustration there. When he sat on the edge of the bed she moved her legs to make room for him. She said 'Why aren't you saying anything in your story about Jesus?'

He said 'I suppose because I don't know how. Or it's all been said.'

'Why did he have to be tortured and killed?'

'I suppose in order to make even the worst things humans do able to seem all right.'

'But they're not.'

'No.'

'They should be changed.'

'Yes. But that's life.'

Evie seemed to consider this. Then she said 'You mean it's a trick.'

'What is?'

'To get people to have babies.'

Adam tried to consider this. He said 'You mean, for life to go on? For people to put up with things in spite of all the difficulties?'

'But they don't.'

'No.'

'Everything should become different.'

'Yes. But it doesn't.'

'No.'

Adam thought – Have I got all this? He said 'But people have to be on their own.'

Evie put out a hand and found his hand on the bedclothes and held it. She said 'I wanted to do something on my own. Not just imagine it.'

He said 'Yes.'

She said 'But I think there's something other than ourselves looking after us.'

'Why?'

'Or things wouldn't carry on. Making no sense. But they do.'

He thought – You mean, like two bricks staying on top of one another?

Then – Sophia? Lilith?

She said 'But I think God must want to be forgiven too.'

'What for?'

'For letting us think he's awful. So we can be awful too.'

Adam thought – But Jesus changed that?

Evie said – 'And perhaps there's a bit of God now inside us too.'

Lilith went to look for the Old Man who should be having his siesta. She found him stretched out at the edge of the precipice with his telescope beside him that was in pieces. He said 'I was trying to see how it works.'

She said 'And how does it? What's inside?'

'Nothing.'

'And what did you think would be?'

'Light.'

'And there wasn't?'

'No. Or yes. I wanted to understand why they don't understand. About darkness. I mean global warming, icecaps melting, sea levels rising. The only difference between this and the last time is that they now do feel they should do something about it although they don't know what.'

'Well that's something!'

'Yes, but they're thinking about how to prevent it, instead of using it to understand how to change themselves.'

'They still think it's somehow some fault of yours.'

'Although they don't think I exist.'

'So then how can they or indeed anything change?'

'Exactly.'

Lilith sat and picked up the end-piece of the telescope and looked inside it. She shielded her eyes. She said 'Is there anything I can do?'

'Well, have a look.'

She took her hands from her eyes. She said 'Nice warm winters, chance of increased food supply, conditions for surplus population at the poles.'

'That'll wow them!'

'You think they won't learn as long as you're around – even though they don't believe you exist?'

'Well I'm quite fond of them really.'

'They'll never do it themselves.'

'But still, I'd better go.'

'Go where?'

'I don't know. Over the cliff. I've had my day. And so on.' The Old Man propped himself up on an elbow and leaned so far over the precipice that Lilith thought he might flop out of his nest like a fledgling, and fly.

Lilith said 'Is this a threat?'

'Yes.'

'Then they won't believe that.'

'No.'

'They'll think it's a trick.'

The Old Man pushed himself back from the precipice and lay on his back again and tipped his sun-hat over his eyes. He said 'They think I don't do darkness.'

'They're trying.'

'Well, they've got to learn.'

Then the Old Man tilted his head and looked at her from under the rim of his hat. He said 'But you wouldn't try to stop me?'

'From going over the cliff?'

'Yes.'

'I wouldn't tell you whether I would or not.'

'So you wouldn't be responsible?'

'Right.'

'You don't think I'd do it.'

'No.'

'You don't think I'd make it?'

'What?'

'Clear the rocks.'

'Oh that! No.'

'So what if I went to one of those places. You know. Where you're assisted.'

'Oh you could do that on your own.'

'All nice and cosy. Hot air and organ music.'

'What have you been watching?'

'There was this chap who was strung up – '

'Oh I know about that!'

'So then they might forgive me.'

'What for?'

'My sense of humour.'

'Now that's a point!'

'You've never noticed it?'

'Why else do you think I married you?'

'Yes that's a point.'

Sophie and her Chinese friend, whom she had at last got used to calling Linn, were walking by the river. He was saying 'I don't want desires; I don't want emotion. I want to feel I know what is the right thing to do. This is often nothing. But I may still sometimes seem to be not just what I am. Does this answer your question?'

Sophie said 'No.'

'Everything necessary has its valid opposite: law and order, mercy and forgiveness. Can one live like this? I don't know. But one has to.'

Sophie said 'I have two friends with whom I was at school. We planned to keep in touch. We thought there might be a way in which friends, being individuals and yet conscious of being connected, might alter the way we look on the world. But one would not be aware of this. Have I said this before?'

'Yes.'

'And you said there is a bit of God inside you that is in touch with God outside you.'

'I do not exactly belong to an organisation.'

'Both you don't, and you do.'

They walked on. It was as if they were on one of those moving walk-ways in an airport that carry people at the same time as they walk.

He said 'I will soon be going away.'

She said 'I thought it would be I who would be going, and you would be staying.'

They were coming to the area in front of the United Nations building which faced the river. Here barriers had been put up and there were police cars, and a helicopter overhead. Sophie and Linn stopped to watch. Sophie thought – What darkness does it take before God has to seem present again? Or – Sooner or later someone will be coming to announce the bombing of Iran?

A policeman came to move them along. Sophie said 'This is where we say goodbye then.' Linn said 'Thank you so much for all you have done for me.' Then to the policeman – 'Have you found the man who tried to fly his aeroplane through the window of his mistress's apartment?' Sophie said 'He's joking.' Linn said 'All right, you go and I'll stay.' Sophie said to the policeman 'We're both going, the same way.' Linn said 'Goodbye then.' Sophie said 'Goodbye.' They stayed where they were. The policeman stopped looking from one to the other of them, and turned his attention to the United Nations building which was what the crowd were still watching but where nothing seemed to be happening.

17

The Old Man and his mistress, the science mistress, were in their car going down to the Sussex coast. Lilith was driving. She had got fed up with the Old Man threatening suicide, so she had agreed to take him to Beachy Head, where he could go over the cliff. He would need some help to get with his wheelchair over the protective fence, but after this he could be on his own. But wouldn't she still be responsible? She imagined he had probably never believed that she would agree to help him – he liked both to be on his own and to have this to complain about – but now perhaps he would find himself faced with the absurdity of a project which had been, of course, less a threat than a ruse to free his power. That would teach him!

They travelled in silence. Earlier, they had had their usual argument about free will. The old man had said – The experiment's failed: they still haven't learnt what freedom is and isn't. The science mistress had said – It's not your fault, they're just stupid. He had said – It shouldn't be difficult to stop being stupid if you realise you don't know anything. She had said – That's too tricky. He had said – There's nothing wrong with being tricky. She had said – Well there's nothing wrong with the wiring.

He had said – There is.

She had said – There isn't.

Lilith had thought – I suppose that's it.

The Old Man had said – 'They don't seem able to do learning unless I'm both out of the way and the way.'

Lilith had said – 'Yes that's it.'

They travelled in silence. After a time the science mistress said 'You talk as if you're God.'

The old history master said 'Are you being funny?'

She said 'That's the question, is it?'

She remembered – There had been mentions of a chap on a motor-bike, someone who took extreme risks. Had it been he who suggested God's gift of freedom to humans could not work unless it included a sense of humour? But his fate had been such a fearsome hazard, that it did not seem it could have been a joke.

They reached the coast, and turned off on the road that ran along the top of the high chalk cliffs. Lilith thought – Looking over the edge will be like peering down the precipice at the edge of the Garden of Eden.

At a high point in the road the science mistress turned off and stopped the car on the fenced-off grass of the car-park at some distance from the cliff-edge. The old man seemed reluctant to get out. He said 'In the old days people drove in their cars over the cliff.'

She said 'I suppose the scrap at the bottom nowadays wouldn't fetch much.'

She went to get his wheelchair out of the boot. He sat in the car and watched her. He said 'And how am I going to get over the fence?'

'In your chair.'

'Are you joking?'

She thought – With any luck.

She straightened the wheelchair and pushed it the few yards to the fence. There she waited. The old man climbed out of the car using his sticks, and joined her. He said 'And where shall we two meet again?'

She said 'In the Bahamas or in Spain.'

He felt that things could not be too bad if she could make a remark like that to him.

But they had difficulty in lifting the chair over the fence. This seemed to be of a height to deter people from climbing it, yet there was no fence cutting off the cliff-edge on either side of the car-park. She said 'You're not trying.'

The Old Man said 'I can't bear to leave you!'

Lilith said – 'You say that now!'

A young man on a motor-bike had turned up just behind them. He revved his engine, making a great deal of noise and smoke. The science mistress thought – About time too! He will now say – Here, let me help you.

He said 'Here, let me help you.'

She thought of saying – I told you!

She said 'You're very kind.'

The Old Man suddenly felt tired. He wished he was back in the Garden beneath his tree. While the others struggled with the chair, he propped himself against the young man's motor-bike which almost toppled over.

He wondered – If one rode over the cliff edge flat-out on this, one might clear the rocks at the bottom and reach the sea.

Such are the uses of extremity.

The young man and the science mistress had got the chair balanced on the top of the fence. The young man said 'Why don't you just take it round the outside of the car-park where there's no fence on the way to the sea?'

She said 'Well why didn't we?'

The old man said 'I suppose we thought it was a cop-out.'

The young man said 'Well that's what I'm going to do on my bike.'

The science mistress was getting the wheelchair down from where it had been on the fence. It slipped and nearly crushed her.

The Old Man said 'I could have got to the cliff-edge by myself if we hadn't gone into the car-park.'

Lilith said 'You wanted to know if I'd try to stop you.'

The young man said 'Are you sure you want to do this?'

The Old Man said 'Do I?'

He was thinking – There was that time in the Garden when Eve came and sat on my knee. I had thought we might have a son. He might come in useful one day.

The young man said 'I can get you there.'

The Old Man said 'That's terribly kind.'

Lilith had been jealous of Eve. She had said – The sooner she's out of the Garden the better!

He had said – Well that was the plan, wasn't it?'

But then, when Adam and Eve were out of the Garden, things had not been quite so clear. Some people had said Eve was pregnant; others that she wasn't.

The old man had managed to push his chair by its handles round to the outside of the fence of the car-park. There he sat in it, and tried pushing on the wheels; but they got stuck on tussocks of grass. He swivelled and faced sideways. He said 'It's hard work on one's own!'

The science mistress said 'What did I tell you?'

He said 'You didn't.'

She said 'I did.'

The young man said 'Here, let me.'

The Old Man thought – I don't know what to do.

The young man said 'I was going to have a go anyway. I had the idea that if I was brave enough, I might clear the rocks and land in the sea.'

The old man said 'Who are you?'

The young man said 'I do tricks. I get up speed and clear an infinite number of statistics or buses.'

The science mistress had joined them. She said 'That's perfectly reasonable.'

With the young man pushing, they left behind the fence of the car-park, and got close to the edge of the cliff. To one side, on the grass, there was an urban-looking public telephone box.

The old man said 'What's that?'

The young man said 'It's for people who change their minds at the last moment.'

Lilith said 'I told you.'

The Old Man said 'You didn't.'

She said 'I did.'

They both seemed for a moment overtaken with laughter.

The old man said to the young man 'Let me go.' The young man took his hands away from the chair. The old man tried furiously to wheel himself, but the wheels still stuck on the grass and he ended up facing in the direction of the telephone box.

Lilith said 'I know who you want to ring up.'

The old man said 'I don't.'

The young man said 'Who?'

Lilith said 'Eve.'

The young man said 'I saw Evie the other day. She was rather the worse for wear. I got her into a taxi.'

The Old Man shouted 'Just get me closer to the cliff!'

The young man said 'I'm going to get my motor-bike.'

The old man and the science mistress waited. It was as if they had done all they could. Then they heard the roar of the motor-bike behind them, and the young man went past them at what seemed to be the speed of light. They could not exactly see if he had cleared the rocks and landed in the water. But anyway he had been like a bird.

Evie was saying 'For God's sake, what's this?' She was holding then pages of Adam's last print-out.

Adam said 'What's what?'

'One can't make out who's who, let alone what's what. Are they the real old man and his mistress, I mean your fictional old man and his mistress, or are they God and his wife you call Lilith, or aren't they fictional too? And who is the young man for Christ's sake? Is he Jesus?'

'I told you I didn't know how to bring in Jesus.'

'You think you're so fucking clever! Are you writing for anyone except yourself for God's sake?'

'I don't know.'

'Oh you're so clever!'

'No I don't think I'm clever, I think it's everyone else who thinks they're clever, who think they know who's who and what's what, what's a story and what's not, what's true and what's not. And I know that I don't know, and what I don't know is the difference between God and humans, and this is a state of grace.'

'All right, I'm not deaf.'

'I mean it's not knowing the separation that is a state of grace.'

'All right. Who's Eve or Evie?'

'I've made you the Virgin Mary, for Christ's sake!'

'We haven't got a son.'

'No, we've got Sophie.'

'Sophie's not the Holy Ghost for God's sake.'

'Everyone's child is a Holy Ghost for Christ's sake.'

'You think it's all to do with us?'

'What?'

'God. Religion.'

Of course it's to do with us!'

'All right, I've said I'm not deaf.'

'Then listen. I'm going to go to Beachy Head and throw myself over that cliff. Have you got it?'

Evie was sitting in the chair that Adam usually sat in. She said 'Are you enjoying yourself?'

He said 'Yes, quite.'

'Well I'm not going to drive you.'

'I can perfectly well drive myself.'

'I thought you're saying we couldn't.'

'Yes, that's true.'

PART THREE

18

Sophie's friend Aisha was a Muslim girl who had recently returned to her home country of Lebanon to see if there was anything useful she could do there. Israeli bombers had done much damage and killed many civilians in the recent conflict in the south, but the carnage at least momentarily seemed to have had some effect. There was less talk now of the intention to obliterate Israel, though Israel itself in general had come to be regarded in a worse light because the savagery had seemed so needless. But Aisha remembered Sophie's father saying that the widespread and tactically senseless bombing of Germany towards the end of the Second World War seemed both to have purged Germans of their addiction to Nazism, and to have made easier the Allies' resolve to help in the process of reconstruction – although the main impulse to do this was the need to make new friends against the new Russian enemy.

Aisha had been intrigued by some of Sophie's father's double-edged pronouncements. He had seemed to suggest that in the centuries-old conflict between Sunni and Shiite factions amongst Muslims, it would be best for outsiders not to act as brokers for peace but to allow the antagonists to slug it out, or even to appear to encourage this – on the assumption that Muslim outrage about this would be the best means of bringing the factions together. But then Sophie's father had seemed to be concerned about the way in which Sophie and her friends had not been shocked by this. He had said – If people start agreeing with me I will have to think up something different: the aim is to inculcate states of mind of uncertainty.

Aisha had wondered how such ideas might apply to her home country of Lebanon, where factions of Muslims and Christians had been at one another's throats ever since imperialist forces had left the area after the First World War. But assumptions and accusations of duplicity had come to seem so natural, that it did not seem that uncertainty needed to be aided by any particular trick.

Aisha had grown up in an orthodox Muslim family in Beirut who professed to despise Christian double-dealing and hypocrisy when compared with the single-minded purity of Islam. But then Aisha had studied the Koran and had tried to come to terms with Islam's own apparent contradictions about the need both for tolerance and mercy, and a ruthless holy war. She had managed to do this more satisfactorily when she went on to study the life of the prophet Mohammed. It had struck her that Muslims, and above all Mohammed, were no more single-minded than Christians but were simply better at dealing with contradictions – mainly by ignoring them. Mohammed, for instance, in political and military affairs, seemed to have been adept at knowing when, for the sake of overall lasting benefit, Allah's call for mercy should be obeyed, and when the demands of ruthlessness. The business of choosing between one attitude and the other seemed to be left to the local leader on the spot.

Before Sophie had left for New York, Aisha had said to her 'It may be that your father's idea of purgation by suffering and guilt is becoming too dangerous. Of course I know your father knows this: it is all part of the trick.'

Sophie had said 'The outcome of which depends on God of course.'

Aisha had said 'Oh well, if you like.'

Sophie had said 'Keep in touch.'

Aisha had said 'I will.'

She had thought – By mobile phone. By super-strings. Whatever.

Aisha did not stay long with her family in Beirut. There was indeed a truce between various warring factions under the trauma of Israel's bombing in the south, but Beirut seemed static in space as if the hurricanes of history were passing over it. Aisha had started on her travels under the auspices of an organisation called *Choice!* the aim of which was to liberate women from male domination in the Middle East. It was claimed that such domination hindered economic growth and thus also political power. The enemies of *Choice!* claimed that by doing away with traditional Islamic culture, the way would be opened to a flood of profitable sleaze and prostitution. Neither side spent much time talking about rights and wrongs; it was felt by both that their interests would be best served by talking about money.

Aisha's funding had got her as far as the port of Tyre, from which she wanted to travel to see for herself what conditions were like in the south. Here she could make her own gesture against the dominance of money! She learned that roads had been rendered unusable by bombing or the threat of mines. So she discarded her Western-style clothes and dressed as a local villager; she bought a donkey with almost the last of her money and put her rucksack on its back and set off walking – she did not exactly know where. She thought – This may be a protest against money and some homage to right and wrong, but what sort of outcome am I expecting to this trick? It is done with an eye not so much to Mohammed, but perhaps to Jesus? Did not Jesus travel about on a donkey? Even if he did say somewhere that he came not to bring peace but a sword.

This was a trick?

The first problem was to get the donkey to move at all.

She headed south-east towards the border with Israel, which she might indeed be prevented from crossing; but then what would she learn –

– Something about the style in which no one seemed to want peace?

She reached a village where people were living in dug-outs under rubble; they expected the bombing to be resumed. They treated Aisha as one of their own: the enemy were men in uniform carrying guns. They told her of an Israeli tank that had crossed the nearby frontier into Lebanon and then had got stuck in a ditch – or rather perhaps in a tank-trap cleverly fashioned from the excavation of an ancient tomb. The Israelis had so far not been able to salvage this tank because of fears of further subsidence of the ground if they sent in heavy equipment. So it was being guarded by a lone soldier with a rifle. This sounded to Aisha like an interesting story: modern technology brought down by an ancient excavation? And what exactly was the story of Jesus' tomb?

Aisha arrived on this scene one evening with her donkey, and stopped at the makeshift fence that had been put up to protect the site of the half buried, half upturned tank. Beyond the fence was the Israeli soldier sitting in an armchair which presumably had been amongst the rubble. He looked so out of place and yet representative of something that had been in the back of her mind, that Aisha smiled and said in English 'You look comfortable!' He said 'Maybe I am.' Aisha took her haversack down from the donkey's back and put it on the ground and sat on it; she faced him through the wires of the makeshift fence. She said 'Were you the driver of the tank?' He said 'Yes.' She said 'Where are the others?' He said 'Gone home.'

She thought – And now you have made this space round the upturned tank your home.

She said 'And what about you?'

'I do not want to go home.'

'Why not?'

'They are mad at home.'

She said 'Yes that is true.'

The donkey was wandering off looking for food. She thought she might let it go.

She said 'In what ways do your people seem mad?'

'They feel they are unique and impeccable, whether they are victims or triumphant.'

'Don't most people want to feel that?' She tried to remember – Does impeccable mean sinless or unable to sin?

He said 'Yes, but most people aren't clever enough to manage it.'

'But it's also a curse?'

'Yes it means that you don't learn.'

She turned to see where her donkey was now. It had found a rubble-littered vegetable patch and was nosing around in it delicately.

She said 'How long will you stay here?'

'As long as it takes.'

She thought – To salvage the tank? To learn?

She said 'Don't you get afraid?'

'I think people find the picture of me sitting here beside my upside-down tank rather reassuring.'

'Its uselessness is encouraging?'

'Well that's the question.'

She thought – And will you wait here till you find the answer?

She tried to see his face more clearly in the dusk. He was young and pale-skinned, with clear-cut dark hair. She said 'What is your name?'

He said 'When we were on the other side of the boundary there was a child, a boy, or perhaps it was a girl, who climbed up out of the rubble somewhere about here and came to the boundary fence and climbed through it and passed by our tanks. I do not know where he or it was going.'

'You didn't stop it?'

'No.'

'You had orders to?'

'Yes. It came from somewhere about here. I wondered why and where.' Then – 'My name is Simeon.'

She tried to remember – Wasn't Simeon that man who sat on top of a pillar?

She said 'So you came across the border in your tank to see?'

'The truce was in operation.'

'Then you went into the ditch?'

'It's not a ditch, it's a tomb, or an underground passage they used to get across the frontier.'

'But this child, or whatever, didn't.'

'No.'

He tried to see her more clearly. It struck him she might be a ghost.

He said 'Who are you?'

She said 'Who was Simeon?'

'He was one of the followers of Joshua who first conquered this land.'

'I'm Lebanese, I was a Muslim, but now I don't really know.'

He thought – And I don't know if we should be in this land.

Night was coming down fast. Perhaps there would be rain. She said 'What do you do when it's dark?'

He said 'I go into the cavern that has been opened up thanks to my tank.'

'Have you got provisions?'

'Yes, we carry them in our tanks.'

'And water?'

'Water is getting low.'

'I have a little water.'

It seemed to him that he was trying to see her through tears. He said 'I would like to ask you to join me, but there are no words for making what I mean sound true.'

She said 'Well that sounds true.'

She picked up her haversack and went to the fence and ducked through it. Her donkey had disappeared in the mist that was rising around the vegetable patch. She thought – A donkey is valuable, it will find a home.

She put her pack down next to Simeon's chair and sat on it. She said 'So here I am.'

He said 'How did you get here?'

'I don't know.'

'We sat for days and watched the bombing. The village was obliterated. Our planes made so much rubble that our tanks could not get through.'

'But yours did.'

'Yes.'

She said 'It's all right now. It's all right.'

He said 'This is our country now. We have nowhere else to go.'

She said 'My people have a tradition of warfare. We seem to have nothing else to do. But recently we have been feeling left behind.'

He said 'Yes.'

The light had faded so quickly it was as if they might have fallen asleep without noticing it. He was saying 'Shall we go down now?'

She said 'Yes, if you like.'

He stood and made as if to offer to carry her haversack, but she shook her head. He left his chair and carried his weapon, and she followed him. At the side of the tipped-up tank there was space to climb down using bits of the mechanism of its tracks as steps. When she and Simeon were under the back of the tank the end of which was still propped on the surface, there could just be seen the opening to a cavern, or tunnel, extending underground in the direction of what Aisha imagined was the frontier. Here there was total darkness.

He said 'Do you mind if we do not have light? I do not have much oil.'

She said 'No. Do you mind if I sleep? I am very tired.'

'I will take you to a mattress on which you can sit or lie, and you can feel with your hands that you are safe in a corner.'

'Thank you.'

His hand took her by the arm and led her half-crouching to where pressure on her arm indicated that she should lower herself. She stretched out a hand in front of her and felt a smooth wall; he let go of her and she lowered herself on to what she could feel, yes, was a mattress. And then there was another wall at the end of the mattress. It was as if she could feel him watching her.

She said 'I'm fine.'

'And you've got your pack.'

'Yes.'

'I will be by the opposite wall, in the corner. I will get some food in a moment.'

'Do not worry about food for me, I will just sleep.'

'As you like.'

'Let me know if you need any water from my bottle.'

'No I am all right.'

'This was where they were tunnelling to blow you up?'

'I think so.'

'Then aren't we lucky.'

19

Adam had gone walking through the streets of London to try to clear his mind. He could not work out if Evie was really displeased at what he had written, or if she was still upset by whatever had happened during her night out. He saw no point in trying to imagine just what this was. He had thought he might say to her – But intrinsically there are bad things as well as good, and if one can accept this, then bad things can sometimes clear the air and be recognisable as good. But this was the sort of thing which, if he said it to Sophie and her friends, they would fall about and groan.

He set off on his long walk down across Oxford Street, into the Park, and thus on his Art Gallery circuit – the Serpentine Gallery, the Victoria and Albert, Tate Britain; then along to the National Gallery where one can have a bit of a sit-down and a cup of coffee. This was the sort of thing Sophie seemed to have been doing in New York. How had she got hooked up with a Chinese guy? The Chinese are supposed to find it difficult to distinguish between Westerners; how does one choose between one and another of them.

Then – I wonder what's happened to that pretty Lebanese friend of Sophie's, what was her name, who looked like an annunciating angel. Or the other one, Amelie, rather more challenging, who wanted to be a reporter on television.

In the Serpentine Gallery there were sculptures of standing or crouching figures whose impact seemed to lie in the spaces between them: not a message, but a recognition of connectedness. In the V&A he went to his favourite oriental section where there were the Chinese Tang horses and the South Indian Chola bronzes of Siva and Parvati, in whom creation and destruction were contained in a single divine figure. At Tate Britain in the big central hall there was an elaborate construction of wires and pulleys with a notice beside it saying *This machine is not working.* There was no indication of whether or not the notice was part of the exhibit. He thought – Well, that's witty.

His journey to the National Gallery took him past the Houses of Parliament, outside which there was a demonstration in progress. Barriers had been erected some time ago to prevent car-bombers getting near the building. In front of these a small crowd was being held back; they were holding banners demanding or announcing *Choice!* Adam thought – You mean, there really is such an organisation?

Then – But I meant it as choice for life.

A hearse had pulled up at the side of the road opposite the entrance to the House of Commons, not far from the back of Westminster Abbey. Two men in top hats were unloading a coffin. Police in yellow jackets were hurrying across the road presumably to tell the men they could not park their vehicle there. Adam had stopped at the back of the group of protesters to watch this scene across the road. He was wondering – How did Guy Fawkes get his barrels of gunpowder into the House of Commons (or was it in those days the Lords?): were they disguised as barrels of beer? That would have been witty. The men in top hats were holding the coffin one at each end and were staring at the police as if they did not understand their language. Adam thought – And perhaps they've got wound-up hair and skull-caps under those top hats; and even nowadays no one likes to open a coffin. Then – But if you drop it, is it wired to go off? Or does it have to be primed when in the House of Commons?

Or even – but surely this was unlikely – Is someone being buried in the Abbey?

A voice behind him said 'Are you Sophie's father?'

Adam turned and said 'Yes?'

The person who had spoken was a young clean-shaven man with only slightly dark skin. He said 'I've been wanting to get in to hear the debate, but the only people they're letting in are Arab-looking men with black beards and skull-caps.' He laughed. He said 'That's a joke.'

Adam said 'Are you Sophie's Chinese friend?'

'No, I'm just wanting to get in to hear the debate.'

'What's it about?'

'Life or death, I suppose.'

'You're nothing to do with that hearse?'

'What?'

Adam turned back to watch the scene across the road. He thought – Perhaps I didn't hear him right. Everything nowadays gets bitten off by gibberish.

The two men had set off carrying the coffin along the pavement in the direction of the Abbey. They were being followed by the police. Adam thought of saying – But it would do you no good to blow up the Abbey!

The voice of the man behind him said 'You're not television?'

Adam said 'No.'

The voice said 'You can get in anywhere nowadays as television.'

Adam felt he should get on with whatever he had been doing. Presumably people were quite often wanting to blow up Parliament. He was on his way to the National Gallery. There he would visit two or three of his favourite paintings – *The Annunciation* by Fra Filippo Lippi, in which a small bird comes down a staircase in a swirl of light to where the Angel and the Virgin Mary are awaiting it; then the small Giorgione *Adoration of the Magi* in which assembled worshippers gaze intently at the ground at what looks like a nest of stones from which the birds have flown. Between these images, or activities, to be sure, there seem to be connections.

In Trafalgar Square the fountains were playing, but nowadays there were no pigeons. He remembered – They have been driven away because it is incorrect nowadays to shit, and yet people feed them. He sat on the edge of a fountain and tried to remember – And what is it about that other painting that I love – the one of the girl with a wound in her throat lying on the ground with a faun at her head and at her foot a dog? Then – But what on earth was that man at the House of Commons up to? He knew Sophie? Perhaps I should try to find her and see if she is all right.

He dialled Sophie's number on his mobile phone. He did not know if its technology reached as far as New York: he did not even know if Sophie was still in New York. Well, what were coincidences, connections, and what were not? While he listened to various buzzings he noticed the strangely beautiful statue of the pregnant naked woman, imperfectly formed without arms, on a previously empty plinth in the square. He had not seen this before; he remembered that it had been chosen to be placed there in preference to what might have been a king or a politician or a general. He thought – There are still miracles!

He said 'Sophie?'

'Dad!'

'I didn't know if I'd get you!'

'Are you all right?'

'Yes I'm fine. Just one or two things that popped up that made me think of you. There was a man by the House of Commons I thought might be your Chinese friend.'

'No, I don't think so. Dad – '

'Yes?'

'Have you heard about Amelie?'

'The one in television?'

'Yes. She went to Iran. She's been arrested.'

'What for?'

'I don't know. She was with a film crew. Can't we try to help her?'

'I'll ask. But she should be all right if she's with a film crew. Sophie – '

'Yes?'

'You don't have to go sticking your neck out.'

'Don't you?'

'No. Let things come to you. They will.'

'Ah, you have to say that!'

'Well you needn't pay attention.'

'No. Dad – '

'Yes?'

He was watching the statue of the naked pregnant woman on the plinth. Why did she have no arms: she could not hold her baby! Was Sophie pregnant?

Sophie said 'Why is everything so terrible?'

'It isn't.'

'No?'

'Look, I managed to get hold of you.'

'Well I'm all right. And you're all right.'

'Yes.'

'So that's all right then.'

'Yes.'

'Give my love to Mum.'

'I will.'

'Let me know if you find out anything about Amelie.'

'I will.'

'See you then.'

'See you.'

'I might just go out to try to find Amelie.'

'Well be careful, won't you?'

A short neat man with a trimmed black beard and wearing a well-cut Western-style suit with an open-neck white shirt came out on to the top of the wide steps in front of an imposing classical-style building above the portico of which there was a frieze in Arabic lettering which, it could be assumed, was a quotation from the Koran. The neat man stopped on the edge of the steps with his entourage of minders, also in Western-style suits, who were spread out behind him like eyes in a peacock's tail. There were a few men in Arab-style white robes and headdresses at one side of the top of the steps, like extras waiting for their cue to come on in a film-set.

In front of the steps was a huge square with a crowd so tightly packed that the heads of persons seemed to be knobbles on the skin of some animal's body rather than of individuals. There was a medley of photographers and a television crew on a raised platform to one side of the square. A group of armed soldiers were crouching almost underneath the platform, as if both to protect it and to be out of reach of its cameras.

The man at the top of the steps began to orate. His voice seemed fragile, because it had no amplification. Perhaps he felt he did not need to be heard. Then as if at a prearranged signal a number of women wearing *niqabs* or full-length veils down to the ground extricated themselves from the block of the crowd and formed a line on their own with military precision in front of the bottom step. Then they pulled their garments over their heads and were revealed wearing T-shirts and shorts. The man stopped orating and looked down on them as if with interest.

The photographers and camera crew on the platform became galvanised like people on a raft in a high wind. They jostled for position, making the raft seem to rock. The soldiers underneath looked up uncertainly, as if they might be trapped and drowned.

Some figures with their faces and bodies traditionally covered by black veils and robes now emerged from the crowd to take hold of the women in T-shirts and shorts either to manhandle them or to pull them back into the crowd. They got hold of their hair and tugged them to and fro as if they were posts being loosened from soil. The women in T-shirts and shorts seemed to be trying to remain upright. However one of them tore at the robe of one of her assailants and there was revealed a glimpse of what seemed to be a male military-style uniform underneath. The photographers and television crew on the platform became like sailors trying to wrestle with a gale. One fell, and seemed to be manhandled by the soldiers underneath.

The neatly-dressed man at the top of the steps raised an arm as if to give an order, and a group of soldiers moved out from under the platform and advanced on the two sets of people struggling at the front of the crowd. But the orders given to the soldiers did not seem to be clear, for on their approach the struggle ceased and those in T-shirts and shorts resumed their formal stance, and those in veils and robes stood around like culprits caught in the act. And the soldiers stood close to the women in shorts looking them up and down.

The person who seemed to be in charge of the camera crew on the platform was a young woman wearing a Western-style headscarf and long skirt. She was shouting 'Keep it going!'

Then as if from nowhere there appeared on the stage as it were at the top of the steps the figure of a young woman, naked, with the body and demeanour of a professional model. She came striding or swanning to the front of the top of the steps and there faced the short neat man who had been orating and put her arms round his neck. She had her back to the crowd. Then she looked round over her shoulder.

The scene was so incongruous that it did not seem that it could be happening.

One of the men in a white robe who had been waiting as if for a cue at the side of the stage now came forward and with something taken from beneath his robe swung a blow at the girl's back or waist – a truncheon? a machete? The girl maintained her pose for a moment with her arms round the neck of the man who had been orating, then sank to her knees. The hitherto motionless entourage of men in suits now swarmed around her so that she disappeared from sight. The man in a white robe who had lashed at her had stepped back. He stretched out his hands to the audience as if to show that they held nothing.

The young woman in charge of the camera crew on the platform said 'My God, I think I know her!'

A cameraman said 'You know her?'

The young woman said 'She was at my school!'

She had no chance to say anything further, because the crowd now erupted into full-scale disturbance, reacting not particularly to what had been happening on or in front of the steps, but lurching about amongst themselves with raised fists as crowds are apt to do who find themselves unexpectedly with a chance to fight. And now the soldiers, as if reacting to instinct rather than to an order, turned their attention away from the crowd back to the raft under which they had previously been sheltering like sharks, and set about dismantling the platform and manhandling the cameramen and television crew and their equipment. The young woman with the headscarf shouted 'Save the film!' but she was going overboard into the arms of soldiers. She was thinking – But it couldn't possibly have been her! What was her name? Then – But I would like to have had a shot of something so original! But by then she was being hustled away and the film had been extracted from the camera. She thought – It would have been a work of art! Even though people would have taken it as propaganda.

Aisha and Simeon had been lying in the dark in the cavern beyond the end of his tipped-up tank. The darkness made everything press close; it was light that made one aware of vast distances. After a time Aisha said 'Are you awake?' Simeon said 'Yes.' She said 'Do you mind if we talk?' He said 'No.'

She said 'Can't you make friends with them?'

'With our enemies?'

'Yes.'

'They don't want us to.'

'They know that you think you don't need to.'

'They say we've taken their land.'

'And you say it's yours.'

'No I don't.'

'But your government does.'

'Yes.'

'Why don't you?'

He didn't answer for a time. Then he said 'Because I'm one of those who think we lost our right years ago when we were not behaving as we were instructed to do.'

'And how was that?'

'We were instructed to obey Jewish law, not impose by force a Jewish state.'

'But once you were.'

'Yes.'

'Do you think God changed his mind?'

'What?'

'When he saw it wasn't working. A Jewish state. All those years ago.'

Aisha shivered. There seemed to be figures lurking in the tunnel that was said to stretch to the frontier.

Simeon said 'And now it doesn't seem to be working again.'

'You still can't share with anyone?'

'So it's said.'

'But if people knew they were in the dark, they wouldn't be able to tell the difference between one person and another?'

'What?' Then – 'But we don't think we are in the dark. We think we've been given a great deal of light.'

'Perhaps that's the trouble.'

'What?'

'If you think you have certainty, then it's natural to see others as enemies.'

'We are the ones who are seen as enemies!'

She said 'I'm thinking about that child you saw coming up out of the ground and moving openly to the frontier.'

'What about it?'

'God must have known he had got things wrong, or he wouldn't have gone to such lengths to put things right.'

'What lengths?'

'A Messiah.'

After a time Simeon said 'But you're not a Jew or a Christian! You're a Muslim!'

Aisha said 'I'm nothing.'

'You're saying it was God who sinned?'

'No no, I'm not saying that!'

She thought – Well what am I saying?

Simeon said 'Oh yes, God might have sinned if he had a son! If he was also man! Or if he was more than one person!' He laughed.

Aisha thought – This is terrible.

She said 'What I'm saying is that it's our sin not to understand.'

The shapes that had seemed to come down the tunnel now seemed to whirl around the room. Then they rushed up and disappeared into the night on either side of the tipped-up tank. She thought – Perhaps they will go out all over the world.

Simeon suddenly said 'Do you want children?'

She said 'Not yet.'

He said 'Why not? Because the world is so horrible?'

She was thinking – That child that he saw might have been using this mattress!

20

When it began to dawn on Sophie that she might be pregnant it did not seem that there was much on a mundane level for her to do. She had not seen her Chinese friend Linn for some time, and she felt she should not be involved with him for the moment anyway.

Their love-making had been such a chancy affair that it must even be doubtful that she was pregnant; she had not been involved with any one else. So it seemed best if things were allowed to develop in their own way. Her father had mysteriously telephoned her as if to find out if she was pregnant, and then had said – Don't stick your neck out. Or hadn't that been about Amelie?

There was a limerick that kept floating into her head –

There was a young girl of Karachi

Who went to bed with a darkie

Di di dum di di dum

Di di dum di di dum

One white one black and one khaki.

This was something that her father had come out with one evening when he was drunk; he had been contending that one could get away with any vulgarity in a limerick. Her mother had said – Not with me.

Sophie now found herself ruminating – Wouldn't it be quite sensible to have triplets? They could share any workload.

– How are triplets formed? Three sperms break into one egg? One sperm manages it with three eggs?

Her father would be likely to say (and not always when drunk) that questions like this were akin to theological ones about the nature of Jesus and the Trinity. And if her mother continued her protestations, her father would say – Don't you think God has a sense of humour?

And Sophie wondered – Shouldn't it be natural for things like this to float into one's head when one was pregnant?

– One felt, after all, that one's child should have a dash of divinity.

Sophie liked to think of herself going on a journey into her own mind and body, sending messages down to her womb – Now look, we don't just want the same old boring characteristics on those strands of sticky tape: the world's getting too dangerous. Can't you come up with something new? I'll try to help, of course, like some old Lilith. But it's really up to you.

Or – What on earth could have been those two lost lines at the heart of the limerick?

Sophie was eager to leave New York. She and Linn had never fitted in, perhaps had even come under suspicion. She thought a practical journey with reference to her mind and heart and womb would be to travel to the Middle East and try to find out what was happening to her friends Amelie and Aisha. It had been reported that Amelie and her camera crew had been released from arrest in Iran, though their equipment and films had been confiscated. They had then disappeared. Their case was being investigated by the British consul in Damascus.

Aisha had said she wanted to act as an emissary for peace between Lebanon and Israel, but her mobile phone had (surely unsurprisingly, Sophie thought) become out of range or stolen or broken.

Sophie liked to fantasize – We three might be seen as some sort of triplets or Trinity? Aisha's family are Muslim, Amelie likes to claim some obscure Jewish forbear, and my father and mother and I go to Church at Christmas and Easter. And oh yes, I would like my babies to have something of both the divinity and the humanity of Jesus.

So she travelled to Damascus and was told by the British consul that Amelie had been to him recently to make inquiries about a visa to Iraq. Sophie said 'I thought it was Iran!' The consul said 'It seems she had a protector.' Sophie said 'You make him sound like a cricketer.'

– Anyway, not like that unfortunate man in my father's story who was having his balls torn off.

But then – Do jokes like this really have to keep coming into my head?

She did not wish to hang about in Damascus; she wanted to settle for a time in a place where there was more of a mixture of religions, and a library perhaps where she might learn more about the theological arguments in the early centuries AD which her father claimed were so important. He used to say – Previous gods, Greek or Egyptian or Teutonic, were no different from animals or primitive humans; so of what help were they for humans to learn to be agents in evolution? And the God of the Old Testament was a fearsome disciplinarian who did offer kindly reassurances but these never seemed to be fulfilled. Then Christians however saw God and Human become One, and then a Third for good measure, to make working relations possible between the Two. Quite simple. What could be more practical?

So Sophie moved on to Aleppo, in the north of Syria, where there was a museum and a library and a settlement of various denominations of Christians – each, she gathered, with their own interpretations of the intricacies of Christian theology. (Her father would say – Truth emerges from the spaces between a variety of interpretations.) And there Sophie stayed for a while, uncertain about but wishing to guard her potential pregnancy.

For might it indeed not be that a new type of human was required? Was it not scientifically correct that although mutations in evolution occurred by chance, humans might have a hand in creating an environment in which one chance mutation might have a better chance of survival than another?

Or what about mental environment? As represented by the messages that Sophie sent down to her womb.

In the Christian quarter of Aleppo there was a museum in an elegant eighteenth-century house that epitomised the luxurious style of living at that age – with no separate quarters for women as there were in Muslim houses. In the museum there were relics and accounts of the life of St Simeon Stylites, the ascetic who in the fifth century AD had lived for forty years on top of a nearby pillar. He had wished, he said, to be able to concentrate on the important question of the relationship between God and Man, and the top of a tall pillar seemed a good place to do this. He did not sit or lie down on the top of the pillar, so contemporary accounts recorded, but spent the time with his arms raised and often standing on one leg. Huge crowds had flocked to gaze at him and to hear what he had gathered about God and Man. When he wasn't praying or contemplating he would talk quietly to men on the ground and they professed to be greatly illumined about matters of such importance. But he refused to have anything to do with women.

Sophie thought – All right, this sort of thing may suit men in their airy-fairy relationship with God, but women surely have to get on with things.

Sophie set out to visit the church which had been built around where St Simeon's pillar had stood. In the bus she outlined in her mind a letter to her father – I see the vitality of the question about the relationship between God and Man, but aren't you giving an answer to it yourself if you go and stand in the air? What's necessary surely is to discover a relationship that will help one to know what to do from one moment to the next in ordinary life on the ground – to know, that is, in terms of 'right' and 'wrong' – and not just for oneself but in recognition of other people, not just in terms of one's prejudices and predilections, nor of one's genes or DNA, but with the sense of some total requirement. Shouldn't this involve the relation between God and Woman? Anyway I'm off to the place where St Simeon stood on top of his pillar, and then I'll see what turns up. This is how scientists work, isn't it?

The landscape she was passing through was of pale rock with patches of reddish soil like spillages of blood. There were occasional ruins of dwelling or shrines like the skeletons of dinosaurs. She thought – This is what much of the world may look like when the heat has come and gone, the floods have evaporated, and an environment is left for other species to be at home in.

She had left the bus and was climbing the hill at the top of which, she read in her guide-book, there was the now ruined church that had been built on the site of St Simeon's pillar. She suddenly began to wonder if she was wearing the right clothes: she was in shorts and a T-shirt and had no hat, although the sun was strong. Also she was walking barefoot – the result of a sudden invasion of humility or perhaps of pride in Aleppo. She had decided – I am on my way to a Christian shrine, I should appear as a Christian pilgrim or penitent, although I realise that this is now a Muslim country and I might cause offence. But so be it. However now I remember that St Simeon couldn't stand the sight of women, especially I suppose those who might be considered half undressed. So – so – isn't it too late? What on earth will be the end of this sentence?

– Why not something about the relationship between God and Woman?

The church at the top of the hill was in the shape of a cross with high interlocking Byzantine arches, most of which were still standing, but no roof. Sophie tried to make herself pay attention to the details of the architecture – the delicately flowing carving on the capitals of the columns, the patches of mosaic on the ground that were like flowers uncovered from snow. But she found it difficult to look at what was around her when there was so much going on in her head.

– If the dual nature of God and Man was contained in one person, then what was the nature of Woman as bearer and nurturer of God-and-Man? If she, Sophie, was going to have a child or children, how was this to be understood or borne?

She found herself eventually in front of a plinth on which there was a large stump of stone which seemed to have been worn down both by the weather and perhaps the depredations of relic-hunters and iconoclasts until it was now the size and shape of a large egg. She looked again in her guide-book – Yes, this was all that remained of St Simeon's pillar! Then it struck her – If it has evolved into an egg, then shouldn't it require a female to sit or to lie on it to get it to hatch? She was pleased with this.

Of course woman's role was nothing like the antagonism and slaughter that men brought into the world – the glib idea that you can't make an omelette without breaking eggs –

And so on.

Sophie wanted to lie and stretch out her arms and embrace the egg.

Then she felt a terrible pain in her foot. This shot up her leg and body and into her head. She thought she must have been bitten by a scorpion or a snake. And might it not be a result of the stupid pride that had made her leave her sandals in the hotel? She sank down with one elbow on the plinth and clutching her leg tightly below the knee; she thought – I have to stop the poison entering my head and heart. But the pain seemed to be already rising beyond her head and suffusing the sky and falling on the earth like rain. So – This is where I will want to die, but will not have the means to die, because I am not on a pillar to throw myself off. And no one will come to help me because I am improperly dressed. This is hell? Or might someone try to make an omelette of me by bashing my head against this stone?

– This might be funny, yes?

– I came here to learn something beyond and yet also perhaps not quite beyond my control?

The Old Man said to Lilith 'What the devil is she doing?'

Lilith said 'She's fallen over.'

'Should we help her?'

'Yes she's learning.'

'Has she gone over that cliff?'

'Or someone for her.'

The Old Man and Lilith had been getting on more easily since they arrived back from Beachy Head. Lilith had said – You don't seem so worried. The Old Man had said – I should still seem a bit worried. Lilith said 'Did you see what happened to that young man who went over on his bike?'

'I'm sure he cleared the rocks. And the lighthouse too. Wasn't there a lighthouse? There was once. He probably got picked up by a boat.'

'Probably smugglers.'

'You think it should be kept quiet?'

'Well people will make what they like of it.'

'It's not so easy when you're old and in a chair!'

'Oh come on, you did have a go!' Lilith came over and put an arm around him.

He said more cheerfully 'And anyway, they needed a younger man. And someone better looking.'

'There you go again!'

'At least now they'll stop telling me what I think and what I do.'

'You believe that?'

'There'll always be a need for monsters?'

'They never thought you were a monster!'

'You mean, they didn't know that that was what they were thinking?'

'Of course they were in awe of you.'

'And look what they did to him.'

The Old Man went to the edge of the Garden and looked over. The scene below had become rain-swept; they might be back at Beachy Head. He said 'It's all right, he's there.'

Lilith said 'Who?'

'Weren't we talking about Sophie?'

'Perhaps she thought she was at the top of that pillar.'

'Well she's got her ear to the ground now all right.'

Lilith went to the edge of the precipice and looked over. She said 'Ha ha.'

'You like jokes! You used to think I didn't understand women.'

'Oh yes, so I did.'

'I just wanted to make sure that chap had cleared the rocks.'

'Well he has, hasn't he?'

Sophie became conscious that she was lying with her head against a stone. She must have struck it when she fell and became unconscious. The pain in her leg and head had lessened; perhaps she had become paralysed and had lost all feeling. She remembered Linn saying – I don't want to have feelings! I want to know just right and wrong. She said – Anyway thank you, old God, old Lilith.

There was a young man bending over her. He was saying 'Are you all right?' He had bright eyes and one of those fashionable beards that looked as if he hadn't shaved for three days.

Sophie said 'Yes I think so.'

'Can I help you?'

'That would be kind.'

'I could give you a lift on my bike.'

The Old Man exclaimed 'Open water!'

Lilith said 'It's still very rough.'

Sophie became conscious of lying with her head against a stone. She thought – What was that about a young man with a bike?

– But he was here! I would let him carry me!

Adam and Evie lay in one another's arms. Adam was wondering about his scene with the Old Man and Lilith and Sophie: should he make it more banal? Evie was trying to remember what on earth had happened on her night out.

She said 'But why do you think the human race needs a new mutation?'

'Because otherwise it seems likely to wipe itself out.'

'That's not new.'

'But we're losing all sense of right and wrong: they're too tricky. Now it's all money, manipulation, what we can make work and get away with.' Then he remembered that Evie was apt to think this sort of thing a bit tricky, so he said 'They're now injecting human sperms into the eggs of cows.' Though he thought of adding – Nothing new about that, ha ha.

Evie said 'It's not sperm, it's DNA. And that's for the sake of experiment, of which you say you approve.'

'Yes.'

He wondered if he had made it clear in his story that it was God who had made Eve pregnant; so she would be the second Eve, or whatever. He might try a scene in which Lilith tries to get the Old Man to make love once more and make her pregnant in their old age, like Abraham and Sarah. But this wasn't necessary, was it?

He said 'I've got Sophie in my story pregnant and suffering, no not suffering, really; on a knife-edge. Does she think this is a world not to bring children into, or does she think they might be a mutation?'

'Well does she?'

'I don't know. We'll see.'

Evie got irritated when he talked as if he wrote his books in conjunction with some Muse, or destiny. She said 'And what about those other two you were so fond of, those friends of Sophie's?'

He said 'Oh yes?' And then – 'And there's something else I've never told you.'

'What?'

'There's another girl, one of Sophie's friends, in my story. She gets herself killed. I think I brought her in because she reminds me of someone I knew. I mean in real life. She gets killed in my story. I suppose I worry about her.'

'You're not making sense.'

'No.'

'She was a real person?'

'Yes.'

'You feel guilty?'

'I don't know.'

'You behaved badly with her?'

'I suppose so.'

Evie had a sense of claustrophobic irritation. She seemed to be in a dark tunnel with shadows like huge bats flying around her. She said 'Why are you telling me this?' He said 'I don't know.' Then – 'Perhaps I'm trying to find out.' 'Find out what?' 'Why I'm telling you. What happened to her. Why I'm bringing her into my story.'

Evie thought – Well I don't want to tell you what happened on my night out, that's for sure.

She said 'You want me to find her for you?'

Adam said 'She was the boldest of them really.'

Aisha awoke in the darkness of her tunnel and did not at first know where she was, she could see nothing; might this mean that she was dead? She tried to trace back in her mind what had happened, and at first this was like trying to remember a dream: you had it, but if you turned away for a moment it slipped and fell and you lost it, and you never got it back. But memory did return slowly, bit by bit; and then settled, to be considered and evaluated; and it was this that made reality different from a dream.

She had been with that commander of an Israeli tank that was half upside down in a ditch, which he had said was a tomb. Was this really so different from a dream? They had talked, they had not made love. He had suddenly asked her if she wanted children. Wasn't this a dream?

The Israeli man had been called Simeon. She had thought of Simeon as someone who sat on top of a pillar. The Israeli had said Simeon was someone who had taken over Israel with Joshua. Whoever Simeon was, he did not seem to be in the tunnel now. She called his name. There was no answer. She wondered if she had offended him by saying that the Israelite God must have known he had got things wrong, or he would not have made such a big deal of the need for a Messiah. And why shouldn't he have had a son?

In the dark, Aisha felt the walls of the cavern or tomb or whatever it was with her hands. She crawled to the corner where Simeon's voice had come from when he had spoken; there was no one there. And now if she wanted to get out, she did not know which way to go. She should be frightened, or would the darkness protect her?

She moved back and felt for her backpack which had been on

her mattress beside her. She might get some light from her mobile phone. Or would the battery have run out? Or would she be so far underground that she would not be able to make contact with anything.

She would have liked to be able to talk with Sophie or Amelie or with Suzie (was that the other one's name?) to make comparisons with what they were doing. She did not know what had happened to Suzie; she had not known her very well. Suzie had been the one who had flirted with Sophie's father.

Aisha's mobile would not light up. She would have to try to orient herself in this tomb in the dark.

She felt her way along the wall in the direction which she thought should lead to the tipped-up tank and thus to the outside world. But did she want to go to the outside world? The outside world, as she and her friend Simeon had agreed, was crazy.

Of course she and the others had been interested in Sophie's father. But he was so much older. He used to say things to provoke them, and then he drifted away.

Aisha was moving holding her hands out in front of her as if to prevent the tipped-up tank falling on her if she came across it suddenly. Then she rested with her back against a wall. But she must have fallen asleep, because she seemed to have been with Sophie's father and the others and someone was saying (was it Suzie?) – Why not just go out there or in there and kill someone or get yourself killed or something! And Sophie's father was saying – Because you don't know if that would be the right thing to do. And now Aisha was in the dark again, and could not remember – had a scene like that actually happened? Or something like it? One was certain of so little in the dark. And now she could not remember which way she had been facing, would she even be able to get back to the mattress where she had slept? For all she knew perhaps she and Simeon had after all made love, and his sperms were even now working their way up inside her.

She crawled on, but she was not becoming aware of the tipped-up tank above her. If she was going the wrong way she might even have gone past the wall against which there had been her mattress. But then here was her pack, yes, thank goodness, on top of the mattress; but she did not want to go back towards the tipped-up tank because the image of it had been frightening; it had been telling her – what – she was going the wrong way, she should be going the other way, in the direction that led underneath the frontier; and there, and then – was this not what she had intended?

So she picked up her pack and put back into it her phone and whatever else she remembered taking out – what a miracle it was when things were where you thought they might be! – and then went crouching and half crawling, heaving and pushing her backpack in front of her, in what she hoped was the direction to the frontier. And after a time what had been a cavern became a tunnel, yes, because if she stretched her hands out she could feel a wall on either side; and she had to keep her head down to stop it bumping on the roof. And all right, she might be a sperm crawling up inside some tube. How many millions was it that never got through to the egg?

Amelie had gone with her film crew to Iran; or was it Iraq? How many hundreds of thousands of dead would there have to be before there became anything living!

Suzie had used to say things like – Well let them kill a few more hundreds of thousands of one another, and then we'll see.

Sophie would say – But we're talking of what might happen in the mind.

Aisha became frightened again. She thought she heard rustling sounds ahead. Had she not felt shapes rushing down the tunnel during the night? And now it seemed to be eternal night, with rumblings more likely to be those of a tank overhead than of a womb. Then there might be another collapse of the roof of a tomb.

She was crawling, pushing her backpack in front of her like – she got comfort from imagining – a placenta, or whatever it was called, ha ha, all the way not to, but from, a womb. Then suddenly when she held her arms out she could once more feel nothing on either side of her: she was in free-fall, being aborted, disposed of; she felt she should be more frightened than in fact she was; perhaps her backpack, her placenta, would be like a planet that would give her purchase and sustenance in space.

But there was something living and breathing on her left. She must have come out of the tunnel and into a further cavern – where people waited in the dark to be born or got rid of? Or had Simeon perhaps come ahead of her on this way? She lowered herself carefully onto an elbow and then reached out with her other hand to her left; on the ground she found a piece of cloth that covered what – a sleeping animal, a root, a leg? And was it dead? It would be less frightening if it were! What were frightening were the living dead, the killers on the surface with their tanks and bombs and planes that prowled like hungry chemicals for whom they might devour. Who had said that? Sophie's father? It seemed to Aisha that she might have made contact with someone sitting with their legs stretched out and their backs against a wall; dead or alive, or perhaps not exactly either, but pretending to be dead, as half alive people may do when they have been shovelled into a mass grave. But then they might prefer to be dead rather than to start fighting their way out from under the piled rotting bodies and bones? Aisha thought that for a while at least she should join whoever or whatever it was sitting propped against a wall, and get a bit more of her bearings. Perhaps there was a whole line of them making out they were dead and waiting for the moment to come alive – like hopeful mutations? Or might they be the sort of dead who were buried with provisions for a future life, which indeed would be useful for someone in this life now very hungry, as she was herself. So that until the time came when people with knives and implements came to tear at her she would – what? She had no power! But she had vision. It was the people with knives and implements who had power.

She might say to them – Look, I have some special knowledge, some understanding, that I will impart to you if you do not kill me: though what I mean, of course, is that I will tell you anything you like. But that is what you want, isn't it?

Would she however be able to make any sound in this silence? The person beside her did not speak.

She had manoeuvred herself into a position with her back against a wall and her legs out in front of her. All right. The person beside her would be the one, yes, dead or alive, whose leg she had touched; so she put out a hand towards him or her to show that at least she was alive, even if they were both under a mountain of the dead. Then she felt something moving against her hand that was like another hand – or a snake, or a scorpion? She waited while it touched and felt her hand; then she thought – Simeon? She took hold of it gently. But it was a tiny hand, the hand of a child. It returned her slight pressure. She thought – It is that child that Simeon talked about? How could it be! But it is so. So that is all right, I do not know why, but it is so.

21

Amelie with the camera crew of which she was in charge had had some difficulty in getting out of Iran. The story of the women in

Western-style clothes staging a protest, and of the fully-veiled women attacking them, became news around the world – together with the claim of evidence that the veiled figures had in fact been male police in disguise so as to prevent accusations of brutal male chauvinism. Rumours of a naked woman who had appeared as if from nowhere to embrace the very-important-person making a speech seemed so unlikely that it was either not mentioned or knowingly discounted. The incident had begun and ended so quickly, and there was no picture of it, that even those who had thought they had seen it could be persuaded to admit that it might not have occurred. Much more profitable to dwell on, surely, was the story of the soldiers smashing the equipment and confiscating the films of the photographers and television crew who had been given permission to record the speech. To spoil such a good political story for the sake of some fantasy about a naked woman would be – well – playing into the hands of people who said modern journalism was all spin and sleaze and triviality.

Amelie considered telling her version, but not until she was out of the country. She might otherwise be prevented from leaving, and she had the prospect of another assignment that she did not want to jeopardise.

And anyway, what could she say that would be understood? That there had been a performance like those about which she and her friends had used to fantasise at school? But then – Had the man in a white robe been part of the performance? And if so, how?

Amelie's further assignment was to film in Iraq. She had gained a reputation for being a young and beautiful as well as talented and successful film-maker, and so sometimes managed to get entry into places and situations where others were not so welcome. She had got clearance in London and Damascus to go with her crew from

Iran to Iraq, but what she would be allowed to film there would depend on the British commander on the spot. There were reports of a mass grave of an independent Muslim Sufi group having recently been uncovered in a sparsely populated area in the west; this was not making headlines because images of mass graves had become commonplace in recent years. The only pictures of this sort still in demand on television were those for which the Nazis had been responsible during the Second World War. Perhaps these were welcomed, Amelie wondered, because they might be held to justify the mass bombing of civilians for which the Allies had been responsible during the war.

But was it not war itself that humans needed, and failed, to justify?

Amelie got a flight to Iraq, to Basra, ahead of her camera crew. An interview had been arranged with the British commander, to whom she planned to say –

– Look, we are waging a difficult and dangerous war against fundamentalist terrorists, yet the enemy that the fundamentalists are most keen to fight are one another. So why don't we just let them get on with it and save us the trouble? Because this would be immoral? But don't we claim nowadays that morality is best served by looking after one's own interests?

The British commander was a young colonel. He sat Amelie down in front of his desk and offered her coffee. Her presence seemed to amuse him. She thought – Well, he is not gay. He said 'Let me first ask you a question. Is it true, as I hope it is, that women presenters on television are nowadays picked mainly for their looks, since that is all that people look for in television?' Amelie said 'And is not that the sort of sexist remark that I might hope to use against you unless you give me permission to film just what I want?' He smiled and said 'So aren't I lucky!'

She thought – Oh dear, this is going to be all right.

She said 'Why did we go just into Iraq to get rid of one evil dicta-tor, when there are dozens of such dictators around the world? Is it simply, as cynics say, because of the oil? But we're not getting much of the oil, we're enabling it to be siphoned off and make millions for people we call our enemies.'

The colonel said 'I thought you wanted to film the graves.'

'Does a war become justified if there can be pictures of graves?'

'You think war is rational?'

'No. But shouldn't you?'

He stood and walked up and down behind his desk. She thought – He is clever; what on earth can he say?

He said 'You want to film that grave in the west? Have you seen a mass grave?'

She said 'No.'

'When you have, come and see me and ask that question again. I shall look forward.' He sat again behind his desk.

She said 'Will you be able to answer it truly?'

He said 'You mean, will I be able to break away from all the rub-bish that politicians spout and that you and I know is rubbish, but I can't say this because I'm a soldier.'

She said 'I mean can't you say it because you are a soldier.'

'Because I have seen mass graves of women and children?'

'Yes.'

He said 'Well, as I say, come back when you have seen one, and perhaps you will be able to answer the question yourself.'

She said 'Thank you.'

He picked up a paper knife and twirled it around in his fingers. He said 'Look, much of the world stinks, much of it does not. If you do nothing, it will go on much the same. But I think we should make our efforts, we don't know if they're right, but we hope, and do what we can. And God does the rest. Do you believe in God?'

'Yes.'

'It is rare nowadays to say Yes.'

'Yes.'

'It's a way of hope. We need it.'

Amelie said 'And that's what God requires?'

'What more do you want?'

'You mean war as an ethical jousting area?'

'What else?'

At this point he gave a yell and appeared to have stabbed himself with the paper knife. A soldier came hurrying into the room. The colonel said 'Will you please see that this lady and her team when they arrive get the purple-carpet treatment for a visit to those graves? May peace be on all their names. And all amenities for filming them.'

Amelie said 'Thank you.'

'And when you return, you must have dinner with me. There is rather a nice little candlelit cellar that I know. Tonight I'm afraid I have to go out and have a joust on the river.'

She said 'Good luck.'

When the soldier had left the room, and she had stood ready to go, he said 'And you can tell me that story about why your equipment was smashed up in Iran.'

Adam was trying to think what he should do in his story about the girl he had called Suzie who rather to his surprise he found he had brought in. Why had he done this? Sophie and Aisha and Amelie were becoming too assured, too invulnerable? He wanted these three figures to have these characteristics, but someone or something had to be wild, out of control. Suzie would be the person whom Amelie had been reminded of when the naked woman appeared on the steps when the very-important-man was orating. He, Adam, had been thinking of someone who had played a very-important-role in his own life; though Suzie was not her name. She had had nothing to do, so far as he knew, with Amelie and the others; but she seemed to be forcing her way into the story because of what he imagined. Was this how stories fashioned themselves? Was this how life fashioned itself! Certainly there had been times in his own life when he had not seemed in control!

When Sophie had been five or six he and Evie had planned to go with her on a holiday abroad with another family with small children, but then Evie's father had become seriously ill. Evie had said 'You and Sophie go; I must stay. The other children will have an *au pair,* so she will help you with Sophie.' So Evie had not come with them, and he had thought – And I will be paired with the *au pair.*

It was what had happened then that had forced its way into his story? A desire to come to terms with his own anxiety, uncertainty? Well how did things work out in time – in life, in a story?

It would not be sense that was made, no. Connections jumped in one's heart and mind like flashes between incidents, between people. Had the very-important-man been making a speech about ethnic cleansing? Had the naked woman been his mistress?

Anyway, there they were on their holiday, he and Sophie and other family of parents and two children aged five or six; and the *au pair,* the extraordinarily beautiful *au pair* from central Europe. She had a dramatic or tragic history as he soon learnt from the parents: she was a refugee from a country where both of her parents had been shot and dumped with others in a mass grave; and she had been five or six, and had tried to find them. And now he had been married to

Evie for seven years; and now Evie was not here; and the *au pair* was naturally feeling somewhat out of things; and he was feeling as if he were on the edge of some war inside him. So should he not be kind to the *au pair*? Do what he could? Oh, to be sure!

He had stayed behind one evening when his friends the parents went to a casino to gamble, and it had seemed right that they should have a night out on their own. But then the children had not wanted to go to bed, and they went to have supper in a café on the beach, he and the children and the beautiful *au pair*; and it was a fine warm night with stars and a phosphorus sea; and the children had gone to sleep on the beach. And then she had told him her story, the beautiful *au pair* – of her parents who had been shot and their bodies dumped and how she had gone to look for them in the open grave. But there were too many bodies, and anyway they were dead. But she planned to go back to her country one day soon, she said, and kill as many as she could of the men responsible for killing her parents – before, of course, she killed herself. And he had said to her – Don't. And she had said – Why not? And he had said – It will do no good. And she had said – I don't want to do good.

And he had said – You will find something worth living for here.

She had said – What? Who? Where?

With this memory coming back to him Adam was now wondering – Was this why the Old Man took Eve on to his knee? Because there has to be sin if the world is to be bearable? Because sin has to be shared?

– This is what Jesus knew?

They had made love on the hot sand, he and the beautiful *au pair* – (the Old Man and Eve beneath their tree?). With the children asleep or with the chance of them not being asleep, it had seemed impossible not to make whatever might be called love, the terrible world being what it is. This was what Jesus had known – there were choices between impossibilities. Of course there might be tragedy. There often was. Sin was called sin because it had to be kept within bounds – of orderliness and caring. What would be the point – what would be consciousness? – of a world of machinery. Then she had said – I do not want to go back to my country.

He had said again – You will find something here.

She had said – I have found someone here.

He thought now – Oh yes, this sounds like a story!

They had met once or twice in London. After a time he had said – You know this is not possible. She had said – I have known that life is not possible. He became afraid – She may not have to kill the people who killed her parents, but she may kill herself.

He had a letter from the man-friend with whom he had been on holiday – Old man, I don't want to butt in, but do be careful. She is very vulnerable.

He wrote back – Thanks for writing. Yes.

He tried to say to himself – Doesn't God want people who are vulnerable?

It was then that he had begun to feel the presence of an Old Man in the sky who had fixed such appalling predicaments for humans so that they would have chances for realisation and wonder. To accept responsibility? He wanted to say to the shatteringly attentive Figure in the sky – Thank you, Old Man, for giving me such meaning, such joy, such terror.

And to his girl with the golden skin and honey mouth – Thank you for giving me such joy, such hope, such meaning.

He lost touch with what happened to her after that. Had she gone back to her country? His friends did not know.

After a time, she made her way into his mind less. Then when he came to write his story of the naked woman on the steps he felt – There must be someone who bursts like an avenging angel from God's knee!

– Or perhaps she is the person who might have leapt out of that coffin and blown up the House of Commons when I was on my way to see my favourite picture of the Nativity?

Amelie travelled to the west of Iraq and saw the piled-up bodies in an opened grave and thought – Well yes, we have become accustomed to this: bodies so dried or devoured that there is no humanity left, no smell; just the haphazard arrangement into which the limbs of women and children have fallen and which, once rats and maggots have done their work, have become as acceptable to cameramen and viewers as a modern work of art. It is the usefulness of the dead that one cannot bear; the thought of other species enjoying a good meal.

But what about the atoms and molecules liberated and flying off round the universe; can't one get a picture of them? No? Might not this give some hope, some meaning? We have become accustomed to pictures of rags and bones but we have not become accustomed to the moment of death, to dying. We think that our bodies should go up to heaven, not be recycled. This is one of the conundrums you have landed us with, old God, and have not provided us with an answer.

She thought she might say to the colonel when she saw him back at the base – Perhaps this is why people like war: not in spite of the killing-and-dying but because of it. In war killing and dying can seem to make sense. They can be seen as not our fault, not our responsibility, but that of fate, a juggernaut. So even distress may be felt as a triumph of endurance; an achievement.

And might this even be true?

Was it this that that girl Suzie at school had felt about death – that it both was and was not her responsibility? She wanted to spit in its face and get it over with.

Amelie thought she might say to her colonel – You are like people who travel with a refuse lorry and jump off here and there to fill it with bits of bodies while it is still moving and then hop back on. Otherwise there would be just too great a clutter in the streets.

But where or what is the final dumping ground?

Amelie had once had an argument with Suzie about abortion. Suzie had said – You should not kill for convenience, but only because there is or has been evil. Amelie had said – How do you know evil? Amelie had not known Suzie all that well. But she had been a real person, not a figment of imagination.

Now, looking down at the mass grave, Amelie thought – Someone might once have been still alive and trying to get out.

She said to the soldier who was escorting her 'Do you have hatred for the people responsible for this?'

He said 'We don't know them.'

'Would you want to kill them if you did?'

'It's not what you want, is it? You do what you're told.'

'But that's what you want?'

The soldier said nothing.

When she was back with her colonel in his office, he said 'Well, have you answered your question yet?' She said 'I can't remember what it was.'

'Why don't we let people who want to kill one another just get on with it.'

She said 'Oh yes, because we have to try to transcend that sort of thing. I mean nature. Even if we can't quite manage it.'

'By doing the killing ourselves?'

'If it's what we're landed with.'

'Well, quite a bit of nonsense can be made of it.'

'Oh yes. Of dying?'

'Let's go and have dinner.'

She thought – Perhaps I am becoming as tough as that girl called Suzie.

The colonel took her to a restaurant in which he said one had once dined on a terrace overlooking the river. Then there had been rocket fire across the water, and diners went underground. She said 'People at home like dining underground.'

He said 'What makes you do your job?'

She said 'I think in filming I might get a sort of God's-eye view.'

'Control things?'

'Observe. People behave differently if they know they are being observed.'

'They might want to kill you.'

'Yes. As they want to kill God.'

They were told what food was available by a man who looked Chinese. Amelie wondered how he had got here.

The colonel said 'I suppose I do my job because I can get along without too much questioning.'

'But you learn right from wrong.'

'Yes.'

'How?'

'By looking. Listening.'

When the food arrived it was fish that the Chinese man said had been flown in from another country. It did not come from the river, which was poisoned.

Amelie and the colonel sat facing one another across a marble-topped table with ornate iron legs. He said –

'There was a grave in a no-man's-land to the north of here that we came across just after bodies had been piled in – containing the results of some so-called sectarian cleansing. It had not yet been covered over, probably because the killers liked to show off their work. But the bodies had begun to decompose. And sometimes they seemed to be moving as if they were alive, though this was probably rats. And so there seemed nothing to do but fill the thing in. But there was one movement that was like a pulse under the skin – this was my observation – that made me think there might be someone alive beneath the skin and trying to get out, but could not, because it did not have the means. So I had to do something. I had to get in. I did not think I could ask or order anyone else; I mean the bodies were soft, rotting, stinking. So I climbed into the pit.

'I do not know if you have ever had the sensation of a situation like this, but it is one of my worst fears. My legs went down, I tried to prop myself with my hands, but my hands went down too, I mean into filth and terror. But somewhere underneath me there was what I had seen as life. But then my face was going down, I mean into the pit, and if this was the outcome of life, then I would rather be dead, I mean is this not what one longs for in hell? I wished that one of my men would shoot me before I sank any further and it might be too late. But I reached something with my hands that might be an arm or a leg, it was more solid than most, less slippery. And I pulled at it, but I could get no purchase, I was pulling myself further down. But then some of my soldiers jumped in to help me. This was good of them. And we pulled out a boy, about ten or eleven, half dead, but not quite. And I did not know if he had wanted us to save him, or to die, as I had done. The rest of his family were dead. He lived. But I do not know if it would have been better for him to get life over with.'

Amelie said 'He wanted you to save him.'

'How do you know?'

'It's a ridiculous story.'

'Why?'

'You're giving your answer to my question.'

'Which was what?'

'Why don't we just let people who want to kill one another just get on with it.'

'You mean we shouldn't?'

'No.'

'How do you know?'

'Because that's what happened.'

They ate the fish that had not been poisoned because it had been flown in from afar. It was delicious. There was some wine from goodness knows where.

The colonel said 'Why was I telling you all this?'

Amelie said 'Because you wanted me to tell you.'

Amelie was thinking – My colonel would be a good person to have babies with, but this is unlikely to happen.

Aisha, sitting in her tunnel in the dark, thought – Perhaps I am one of those eggs that gets stuck just short of a womb.

The presence that had seemed to be next to her, whose hand she had felt she had held, might have been a non-identical twin? Or someone in a grave, waiting to be helped to come alive again?

But now, whatever it had been, it seemed to have gone. She must have been dreaming again.

She would like to have asked it – You know that child that my friend Simeon saw coming out of the earth somewhere about here – do you think that you and I are something of the same?

But now she had to try to make sense. Even what might have been a dream had been trying to reassure her – This cannot be a sort of catacomb that you have come to because there is no smell. Surely a better idea is that it is the tunnel that people were using to get to and fro beneath the frontier. So if you go on, why should you not eventually emerge and find Simeon in the light?

She stirred, preparing to stand. The people who had seemed to be sitting on either side of the tunnel, whether they had been or not, seemed anyway to have moved their legs. So that was good of them. Or did it matter? Why was the dark said to be frightening: could you not try to make of it what you liked?

She murmured quietly – 'Simeon?' She thought – He might have come this way. He had done what he could for me.

But if she came out into the light, what would she find? Men with guns waiting for her as if she were a rabbit emerging from a hole? Then being blown to bits, so that she would be on a cloud like those mad virgins, or bluebottles above a grave?

Or in a maternity ward, with the masked faces of grown-ups coming down like giant squids. Then either – Put her in the bin. Or – Oh isn't she lovely, the little beaut, brute; she'll soon do what she's told!

Or a landmass in which you are in the arms of gravity, with the care and attention of atoms and molecules preventing you falling through.

She heard voices. She wanted to say – Is it you?

She was coming to the end of the tunnel. There was light. She had almost forgotten how light hurt – how it formed one thing rather than another – that one had to avoid, or to bump into.

Or perhaps a home of gentle hills and a lake and a river that does not run to the sea but rises into the air invisibly.

She – or maybe they, because she was still feeling that she might not be alone – were coming out to where in the distance there was a grassy slope, yes, but the immediate foreground was a crater of rough earth that seemed to have been ripped by force out of a hill. She was on her hands and knees: how white and strong her arms were! She had been trapped, and now was freed! She tried to wipe her eyes, but there was dirt and blood on her fingers. She thought she would say – 'I thought I heard Simeon.'

Someone was saying – 'Simeon?'

There were soldiers around her poking their guns at her. She hoped to say – But I wanted peace. I didn't want to offend you.

Simeon had said – Everyone's mad at home.

She had said – Yes that's true.

The soldiers were talking in a language she did not understand.

Simeon had said – I would ask you to join me, but there are no words for making what I mean sound true.

She had said – That sounds true.

Then she had joined him, and he had told her the story of the child that had not used the tunnel but had climbed through the wire. Should she mention to the soldiers that there might still be children in the tomb?

She could say – I will tell you anything; because it could all have been a dream.

She was being lifted by her elbows. She still could not see very well because she had been so long underground. She might say – Carry me along taddy like you done through the toy-fair. Had this been a voice from the tomb?

The soldiers were talking about Simeon. She was saying 'Simeon, yes, take me to Simeon.' She raised her head because her eyelids were wiping the light clear. The grassy slope went down towards a village. In the valley there were tanks spaced like memorial stones. The child that climbed through the fence had gone wherever it had gone. She had already said, had she not – Take me to Simeon.

What had Simeon meant when he said to her – Do you want children?

In Washington D.C. a press conference was being held which Sophie's Chinese friend Linn was attending. He had not heard from Sophie since she had left New York. He was awaiting fresh instructions from his contacts in Beijing. He sometimes wondered if Sophie might be pregnant.

The press conference was assembled in a room which appeared to be panelled elegantly in wood, but it was said that the walls behind this were of steel, so it could not be said that every precaution had not been taken. But this composition of the room gave to the voice of any speaker a lack of resonance that made it difficult for a listener to be clear about his meaning, so that there was thus a reason for disagreements about interpretation.

At the end of the room which the audience faced there was a wide doorway opening onto a long corridor down which a very-important-person or persons could be expected to come. And now here two were! – swinging into sight at the far end of the corridor like racing motorists coming into the last straight, but to those viewing from head on hardly appearing to be moving. And indeed it seemed that they were taking care that one should not get in front of the other; so the race would not appear to be subject to hazard but to be under political control. The skill was in giving the impression of endeavour, without the chance of things not going to plan.

The two men walked like gunfighters with their arms curving out from their sides, giving the impression of youth or weaponry. Linn thought – And indeed they are children playing aeroplanes or guided missiles. Having entered the room and thus arriving at the finishing line the two men spun off onto a podium on which there were two desks, which in the event of any terrorist activity might provide body armour at least for guts and balls. And if heads were shot off, might this improve ratings? One of the men, now as if in the role of servant, remained upright and smiling and arranged papers on his desk. The other, now in the role of master, leaned forwards nonchalantly with his elbows on his desk as if ready to enjoy whatever humiliation might be offered.

Linn made a mental note – Might much of Western psychology be understood from the much admired story in Proust's novel of the man who likes being beaten and buggered, but in order to maintain his style of satisfaction has to cry Stop! Stop! when he means Go on! Go on! But this is apt to be misunderstood by his bemused servant, who therefore spares him.

– However surely sooner or later some sophisticated executioner will come along who will say – Sorry, I thought it was understood that you didn't mean what you say – and so bang! that will be the end of him.

There was a flurry at a side door on a level with the podium; someone was trying to burst in and was being restrained. The man bending over the desk was speaking charmingly, confidentially, as if he were a comedian softening up an audience before embarking on a more risqué routine. Then someone in the audience laughed and clapped loudly. Security people at the door turned their attention from the man who was trying to get in, to this man in the audience who was young and somewhat dreamy-looking with a wispy beard. He was now looking round as if embarrassed, and pointing to his ear. Was he deaf? Had he been receiving instructions? Was one supposed to have sympathy? The man at the side-door was now gesticulating wildly, as if to warn either the audience or the man in the middle about them. The man in the audience gave another loud laugh, then held a hand up to his mouth and looked alarmed. Linn imagined him saying – I'm sorry, I've got Tourette's syndrome! Or why not just – But I thought the performance so splendid! The very-important-man leaning over his desk had stopped speaking; a group of four or five men from the door were advancing on him presumably not to assassinate him but to hustle him to safety. But which way should they go? The man at the door had stopped struggling. But then someone in the front row of the audience stood up and pointed urgently towards the long corridor by which the two men had entered; but whether this was suggesting an escape route or giving a warning of further danger was not clear. Then it seemed to strike the second not-so-important man who was still standing behind his desk on the podium that he might be taken to be a comedian if he went on smiling, so he looked stern; but then might he be taken to be a target or a terrorist? The man in the audience who had laughed and clapped was now being set upon and pinioned by people in seats on either side and behind him. He reacted as if he were being tickled, whooping and gurgling. Linn wondered if he should go to help him, but he seemed to be doing all right on his own.

22

Sophie was lying with her head against the stone that was like an egg. She thought – But I have been here for some time. Had she been to sleep again? The pain had gone from her leg, though it seemed that she might have lost the use of it. She thought – But still, no pain is a mercy. Someone had come and offered to help her, and had talked about a bike. She had said – That's extraordinarily kind! He had reminded her of someone in a picture somewhere. And there had been the sound of laughter. Her head seemed to be stretched to its limits;

but if she stayed still, its contours might not collapse. She had been asking the man on top of the pillar about the relationship between God and Woman. Then she had fallen and hit her head against this stone. Or had the man on the pillar pushed her? He was said not to like women. Then the one who had offered her a lift had come and gone. He had seemed so fragile himself! But perhaps he had to be if he was some sort of magician. She sent a message down to her inside to ask if her babies were all right. It seemed there was no reason they should not be.

Now another man was standing over her. She was saying 'No I'm all right.' This man wore a long white cloak or robe, and an elaborate headdress in the style of a woman who has had her hair washed and set. He said 'What happened?' She said 'That's what I was going to ask you.' She thought – I can't really say I fell both off and onto this pillar.

He said 'Here, take this.' He seemed to be struggling to remove some garment from beneath his cloak.

She said again 'No I'm all right.'

'You can't go around like that.'

'Like what?'

'Did someone attack you?'

'I don't think so.'

'I wouldn't be surprised.'

He had succeeded in producing a length of cloth like a cummerbund from beneath his cloak. She thought – I wonder where that has been! He held it out to her.

She said 'No really.'

'You've got to cover yourself.'

She thought of saying – Am I inflaming your lust? Or even – Is that one of the relationships between God and Woman?

She said 'Can't you give me your robe?' She laughed.

She was sitting up on the stone with her feet on the ground and her knees apart. She took the piece of cloth. She thought – I'm a bit of trouble and strife.

He said 'I will take you to my uncle's house and get you some clothes.'

She thought – He is extraordinarily good looking! Will we go by camel or Rolls Royce?

She got to her feet. She said 'Why do you want women covered up? You feel them a threat?'

He said 'Can you manage?'

He moved off through the shell of the church with people making way for him. She thought – He must be used to people following him without his having to look round. Then – But it's true I want to provoke him.

She said 'Where does your uncle live?'

'In Aleppo.'

She didn't say – But I've got my own clothes in a hotel in Aleppo!

She said 'Are you married?'

'Yes.'

'Are you rich?'

'Yes'.

'You can have half a dozen wives?' She laughed. 'I do see the usefulness of that.'

She tripped along behind him, stumbling both on the leg that had gone to sleep and over his piece of cloth she was trying to wind round her.

She said 'But what are you doing here? What an odd place for you to be!'

She thought – Well he won't say, will he, I noticed you getting on the bus and followed you all the way from Aleppo.

'Why odd?'

'A Christian shrine! A monument to a man who sat on top of a pillar.'

'For the most part he liked to stand and be in a certain amount of pain.'

'So what are you doing?'

'I was checking a project we have. To build a new pipeline to the sea.'

'A pipeline for oil?'

'And gas. We have plenty.'

'So where do you come from?'

'I have many homes. I own the house where my uncle lives in Aleppo.'

Sophie thought – The trouble with that man on top of the pillar was that he could not move. The trouble with this man is that he thinks as long as people are correctly dressed, he can go where and do what he likes.

Then, having got the length of cloth he had given her wrapped becomingly around her, she thought – But what can I learn?

– I came to ruminate on the relationship between God and Woman, I found myself where that man had got stuck up on his own pillar – how on earth did they get him down; with the sort of equipment they had used to build the pyramids? But you don't get close to God by building a tower, you get close to God by becoming the sort of person that God is – that is, a creator or procreator, and giving children the chance to go their own way, from the learning they have got from you. And thus you keep close to God and God keeps close to you. Isn't that what you were getting at, old goda-daddy, when you were writing about the Old Man and Lilith? But then you get Eve to sit on the Old Man's knee: why did you do that, old bonkadaddy – to bring into the story the second Eve? To show the Holy Ghost as a woman? Well, I am a woman. So what are you doing now, young Linn?

– Did I never tell you that I might be pregnant? But we were not each other's sexual type, were we, you knew that, we were too much alike, we had peace. But procreation is a bit of war, is it not; things are apt to stay the same in peace. But what if I had triplets – one white one black and one khaki – they would be the same and yet not, wouldn't they; I mean from the same womb but not from the same sperm or egg, that sort of thing. And then call it war, call it peace, what you like. It would be a bit of a lark, wouldn't it? I mean a bird. The sort of creation about which when the curtain comes down and people stand up and cheer, you would still be behind the curtain, would you not?

– So if a bit of evolution's still wanted – well here I am, old Linn, rambling along about ten steps behind my terribly handsome Arab friend who likes everything and everyone to be in armour from top to toe because he thinks all is at war and you have to be in control. But who in fact might be the lucky father then? And might the others never know? You'd get chopped up if they did! But Nature's model agency needs a bit of a try-it-on here and there. So here I am, young Linn. I'll see you later. Whatever will be will be: I mean yours, truly. So – so what? Don't ask. Unfasten your seatbelts, boys, we're in for an interesting evening.

The plan that Sophie's Chinese friend Linn was supposed to be promoting, he had understood, was that when the right time came the Chinese would supply extremist Islamic movements in the Middle East with such nuclear or chemical or biological material as would enable their agents to plant bombs of this nature when and where they chose. Linn also understood that there were scenarios to make it seem that such catastrophes would have been caused either by accident, or – with scarcely believable deviousness – by the victims themselves. Linn had asked his superiors for elucidation about this last bit of flapdoodle (he had just learnt this word) and was told – It is now generally understood that in the course of human history civilisations that have run their course bring about their own destruction. Linn had said – Yes, but don't they know this? It had struck him that the idea might have been a joke; but whether it was or not he did not want to seem to be naïve about it.

There had been the question of who would have ultimate control of such weapons, the Islamists or the Chinese. But this question could acceptably be sidelined if it was generally suspected that such weapons did not exist. And indeed all those concerned could enjoy much more effective freedom of plotting and braggadocio (another word Linn was pleased with) if in fact they did not exist.

And if humans were mad, would it not be helpful to help them to see they were? This, Linn argued to himself, was the justification for his own attitude.

Linn was not at a high level in the hierarchy of Chinese Intelligence, but his relationship with Sophie had enabled him to concoct some reports (conceivably gleaned from British Intelligence?) which he had hoped might both be generally helpful in diverting attention from what might otherwise grow into genuine and serious crises, and keep him in favour with his own people. And he had been gratified to find his superiors commending him – though of course they would have their own reasons for doing this. He had explained to Sophie – When I say one has to let things take their course, I mean this is the sort of course that things take. She said – You mean they will either ignore you or have you eliminated?

But the style of the secret world of Intelligence was coming to seem to Linn to be such that people were seeing one another almost literally as 'spooks' (ah the shrewdness of words!) – that is, as beings of no substantiality but with the power to convey alarm and possibly entertainment. Their task might be to provide 'cover-ups' – and so what if it was known that the cover was a white sheet from a bed? Linn ruminated – Intelligence people like to keep truth covered in the way that Islamists like to keep women covered, because uncovered each constitutes a threat that cannot be controlled. But then it is truth, yes, that takes its own course.

And among Linn's people the idea had recently been growing that it was becoming scarcely necessary for them to promote stabilisation, destabilisation, or whatever balance between the two, because Natural Forces were taking on the job for them. How long, was it now being said, before New York and London could be expected to be under water, while Beijing and Chengdu (surely not!) might not be (Linn must look this up). Most Westerners seemed remarkably sanguine about this; so was it true they were ready for self-destruction? Sophie, he remembered with nostalgia, would have added – Yes, and thus with the chance of self-renewal. And he, Linn, would have added – But that is what people in the East more naturally think.

But what did Islamists think? Linn gathered that specialists in China had been put on to the study of Islamic texts to ascertain what might be seen as the will or opinion of Allah in this respect. Nothing clear-cut, as usual, had been gathered from the Koran. And from stories of the life of the Prophet it seemed that Allah saw the way of advancing his interests was to take the best advantage that any situation seemed to offer. And for this Natural Forces seemed as well suited as spooks. The evidence for global warming was so scattered and contradictory, that is, that politicians could make what they liked from it in the manner of students of the Koran.

Linn found himself somewhat lost though not particularly disheartened by all this. He longed to be with Sophie again, who had the gift of being at home in the maze and trickery of both words and things.

He wondered – But why was it so difficult for Sophie and me to make love? We knew we might have a child?

– A child would have been an instruction for us to stop getting satisfaction from all this nonsense?

He did not know how to get in touch with Sophie. She was not answering her mobile. He thought – Please God, let her not have come to any harm.

The summer was hot, and on television there were pictures of ice melting at the North Pole. There was a film of a polar bear stranded on a drifting ice-floe who had to swim for miles to find food, and then was too weak to snap the head off a walrus. Then there was an inexplicable advertisement showing a small child naked except for a nappy abandoned on a small piece of ice-floe, and looking alert and not too discontented. What on earth could this be intended to promote? Would Sophie say – global warming?

Linn felt a great weariness come upon him. Sophie and he had felt they had a task to try to change the world. But what did it matter if the human race was wiped out? Humans had had their chances, made their moves; but their creations or procreations were monuments to death, not life. The best way to look at the past, Sophie had said, is to be able to make a joke of it. But what of the future? Can you think of a joke about a baby abandoned on an ice-floe?

Can seeds in fact float for thousands of miles on ice?

The Old Man, standing at the edge of the precipice with a hand on the small of his back as if he had become paralysed by sudden pain, said 'What the devil is that baby?'

Lilith, who was lying on her stomach looking over the precipice with her opera glasses, said 'I think it must be part of their latest production of *The Icecap That Came Down from The Pole.*'

'But why the baby?'

'That's what they've come to think babies are for.'

'What?'

'Making one feel all tragic and concerned, but without the chance or need to do much about it.'

'They may wipe themselves out?'

'It's possible.'

'Do you think I should come out of retirement?'

'Please! No! They can perfectly well do it themselves.'

'I mean, get it over with quickly. They've become so incompetent. Silly.'

'It didn't work the last time.'

'I didn't do it the last time!'

'No, you put a load of babies on an ice-floe. I say, do you think that's it?'

'What?'

'That's what they're doing now themselves! That baby on an ice-floe.'

'Who, those girls?'

'Yes. In their minds. Unfreezing. Turning into activity.'

The Old Man tried to straighten, but his back evidently still hurt him. He said 'Well the baby looks contented.'

'Can you see any others?'

'No.'

'There should be at least three.'

'Girls or babies?'

'I don't know.'

'Well we'll have to see.'

The Old Man tried to lower himself to the ground gently; but then lost control, twisted, and landed on his back rocking to and fro with his arms and legs in the air like a baby.

Lilith watched him. She smiled. She said 'You'd like it all to be you.'

'And you!'

'And that chap who went over the cliff. Where is he now, do you know?'

'He's always on the move. He got the message about not staying at home.'

'But what about that trimmer with a beard.'

'They've all got beards.'

'The one who doesn't like his picture taken.'

The Old Man seemed to think about this. Then he said 'They think it's just with a passport they can get up to heaven.'

Lilith seemed to think about this. Then she came and sat by him and put a hand on his knee. She said 'One thing I've always liked about you is your sense of humour.'

He said 'God help them.'

Lilith propped herself on an elbow and looked over the precipice again. She said 'Look, there's something interesting happening.'

Raising his arms in the air again as if he were a baby on an ice-floe, the Old Man made shapes with his fingers as if these, blocking the light from the sun, might form shadows against his eyes. He said 'You think those girls will manage it?'

Lilith said 'Oh well, they'll try.' Then – 'Look! She's getting into his Rolls Royce! Or is it a camel. Anyway, he'll be taking her to Aleppo.'

Evie, lying on her front on a mattress in their small back garden, was reading pages from Adam's typescript. Adam came out from the conservatory. She said 'You seem to be getting everyone and God all joined up.'

Adam said 'Isn't that what they should be?'

'By the one who went over the cliff?'

'Oh well, if you like.'

'That wouldn't stop them fighting.'

'Oh well, they may be able to get up and take a bow when the curtain comes down.'

'In their minds?'

'Oh, in their minds.'

'And then?'

'I thought I might make that Chinese chap start getting things right. But what's the evidence. It would have to be tested.'

'The evidence for what?'

'For being able to know right and wrong apart from self-interest or dogma. Or what is true self-interest. Apart from words.'

'Well how do you test it?'

'Perhaps like this.'

He sat down beside her and put his hand on her behind and moved it around as if he might be kneading dough.

She said 'How many times have I told you not to do that!'

He said 'About a hundred.' Then – 'Just testing.'

'Haven't you learnt that the result is always the same?'

'The scientist lives in hope.'

'Of what?'

'That his conjecture may one day be verified.'

She rolled over on to her back. She said 'But your conjecture is verified. You think it will annoy me, and it does.'

'So then what?'

'I suppose you're testing your theory about sexuality.'

'Not so much sexuality.'

'Then jousting. Warfare. Peaceful warfare.'

'Right.'

'Creation, procreation. Whether or not sexuality.'

'Got it.'

She held out her arms to him. She said 'All right, leave it to your girls.' Then – 'Here and now there may be people watching!'

Sophie and the Arab man had gone to what he called his uncle's house in Aleppo and there they had made love without much bother. Before they had begun Sophie had asked the sort of questions that she had understood it was proper to ask in New York, and he had said – 'We're not like you. We see the advantage in having a lot of babies.' And then – 'If necessary I can make you one of my wives.'

She said 'Supposing I don't want to be?'

'You may find I have other attributes apart from being very rich.'

Afterwards he said he had to go off on business. She thought – Ah yes, that's always welcome.

Before he went, she said 'Can I ask you something?'

'Yes.'

'Would you have preferred it if I'd fought you tooth and nail?'

'No, that would have been unproductive.'

'Wouldn't you like something new?'

'No, what's the point?'

She wondered – What is it if it isn't boredom if you always get your own way?

When it seemed that he had left the house she went out into a courtyard of such glittering elegance that it seemed to be trying to make her eyes look away. In the middle was a small pool with a fountain playing. The fountain made a tinkling sound which made her want to pee. There seemed to be no one in the courtyard, so she thought she might do it in the fountain, but the architecture was of arches and pillars from behind which there might be people watching. She thought – Those women in long black robes, is it easier for them to pee?

There did not in fact seem to be anyone anywhere in the building. There must be servants? They kept out of sight in case anyone got up to no good?

But there must be a bathroom somewhere.

She went back into the bedroom in which she and the Arab man had made love. A table had been wheeled in with things laid as if for breakfast, although by this time it was late evening. There were baskets covered with napkins and pots with silver lids. Did her Arab friend think he controlled the ordering of time? Or was this the bedroom of one or another of his wives?

There were croissants and butter and marmalade, and what looked like gulls' eggs in their shells. And both tea and coffee.

And there was a bathroom next door with a bath with taps in the shape of swans' heads. She thought – So one might feel like Leda with her swan. When she was sitting, with relief, she tried to remember how she had got here. She had wanted to inquire into the relationship between God and women. Was she now one of the forty-odd ex-virgins that are said to await every hero in heaven?

– Or was it the role of women in relation to God to win by losing, as Linn and her father might say?

She went to wash her face. Above the basin there was a cabinet on the outside of which there was no mirror such as there might be expected to be in a Western country. She thought – They don't like seeing themselves? This might stop them getting up to heaven?

She opened the door of the cabinet and a light lit up inside. A face stared back at her of such alarming intensity that she wanted to say –

Sorry! – and to shut the door quickly. It was a round face with good cheekbones and bright dark eyes and hair forming a frame; a nose and mouth like openings to the light that seemed to come from behind the eyes. She thought – My God, is that me? I didn't recognise you! Sorry! Then – All right, yes, I'm doing what I can.

She thought she would go and lie on the bed. But she should have breakfast or supper or whatever it was first – not only because of hunger, but out of gratitude to her Arab friend and respect for the servants who had so thoughtfully kept out of sight. Recently she had not had much respect for her own body, but if others were attentive to it, why should not she be? She ate quickly some croissants and butter and honey and drank both tea and coffee. She wrapped some gulls' eggs in a napkin and put them by the bed. Then she lay down. She thought – And when I wake up, I suppose the table with the food on it will have mysteriously gone. And I suppose this whole magnificent setting may have gone, but I will have had the impression that I had something to do with it.

23

Aisha went with the soldiers down the hill on the path where she felt Simeon must have gone. She thought – This is what I have wanted. But I am not in love with him: so why am I doing this? What is taking over from the compulsions of love or resentment – the need to do what seems required?

The village or small town at the bottom of the hill was a settlement of modern concrete block buildings placed like huge bollards at the edge of traditional village-type housing – but with the intention, it seemed, not so much of preventing movement as to give notice that any movement would be watched. At the side of the village which she and the soldiers were approaching there was an open space with goal-posts and a primitive stand for spectators. On this site were the stationary tanks which Aisha had taken note of from the top of the hill, and which were like components of a war memorial. In front of them was a group of half a dozen Israeli soldiers who seemed to be restraining one of their number from addressing a small crowd of villagers who had gathered in front of the stand for spectators. These were dressed in the working clothes that marked them as local Palestinians. The soldier who was being held back, Aisha realised, was Simeon. She had not seen him clearly in daylight before.

The soldiers escorting Aisha had stopped. They indicated that she should not come any further; she should stay on the dusty slope with one soldier to guard her, while they went down to join the group by the tanks.

Aisha thought – That is right. I will be able to watch whatever goes on as if it were a stage-play.

Simeon was shouting in the direction of the small crowd by the grandstand. Then one of the soldiers holding him hit him with the butt of a pistol in the face. Aisha wanted to shout to Simeon – But just stop shouting! Simeon had bowed his head and seemed to be sinking to his knees, but was being held up by his elbows. The villagers looked on silently. Aisha rather hoped that someone would start firing. Then she could run down the slope towards them.

She would say – But if you are saying that he deliberately sabotaged his tank by driving it across the frontier and then on to the weak part of the tunnel so that it collapsed and exposed the secret access into Israel –

– That is correct?

– Or are you saying the tunnel is yours?

– But that child did not use it!

– And anyway, it was an interconnected system of tombs.

Simeon was no longer shouting. Aisha wondered – What precisely was he telling them?

– If she walked down the hill now she might join him?

– They don't have the death penalty in Israel?

– At least not for their own people.

– We might be together in solitary confinement?

She needed at least to let Simeon know she was there. Then they might go their same or separate ways. And with luck not in a dungeon. She might tell him she might be pregnant? It could be that he too could not remember clearly what had happened the night before. In the dark, anything had seemed possible.

The figure of a child, a young boy or girl, was emerging from the crowd in front of the grandstand and was approaching the group of soldiers holding Simeon. Aisha thought – Well yes, why shouldn't that be the child you talked about, that climbed through the wire? And what was that poem you said came into your head; or was it into my dream?

The child was standing in front of Simeon. The soldiers and Simeon were watching it. Aisha wondered – Will they now let Simeon go? Then – How ridiculous! Anyway, where would Simeon go?

Simeon straightened and raised his head. One of the soldiers holding him took a cloth and wiped at the blood on Simeon's mouth and chin. Then the others let go of him.

The child began to move on. It was crossing the playing field in the direction of where Aisha was sitting on the hill. It was not as if it had seen her. But Simeon, watching the child, surely must now see her! She was still being guarded by the soldier on the hill. Then Simeon gestured towards this soldier, and the soldiers around

Simeon turned to see what this soldier would do. The soldier slung his weapon over his shoulder, looked briefly at Aisha, then set off down the hill.

Simeon and Aisha were now observing each other. Aisha was saying to herself or to him – Oh this is good, very good; now hold it! Hold it! The child must not take note of me, must go past me, as it went past you in your tank. But I will have seen whether it is smiling. After that I don't know. What does it matter. We will have been involved in a bit of – what do you call it – think of a word for it – or that is not necessary.

Evie said 'For God's sake, what's this? The child is now supposed to be Jesus?'

Adam said 'It can be what you like. Choose your word for it.'

'Children don't just go wandering on their own in and out of a battlefield.'

'But they do. Don't they have to? Better recognise it. Get used to it.'

'You're not talking about domestic quarrels, you're talking of war.'

'What's the difference? I mean in the use that might be made of them.'

'By children?'

'Why not? Who else has even a chance of not being trapped in conditioning?'

Adam was feeling exhausted. He seemed to have come to the end of what he could write. There were times when he wished Evie could help him more with his work, then times when he was grateful to her for leaving him to himself. But in all this, he recognised, he was glad to be able to move between one state of mind and the other.

He said 'I mean, isn't everything what we make of it? And if we happen to make of it what happens, then that's what it is, yes.'

'And the rest is word-games?'

'Yes.'

'But isn't what you're playing word-games?'

'But saying Yes to that isn't a word-game.'

'Why not?'

'Well it either is or it isn't.'

'You used to say you and I couldn't talk about things.'

'But we can now.'

'Even to say there are things we can't talk about?'

'Right.'

'So what happens now?'

'We're talking about things.'

Evie looked exhausted. But it was not with the exasperated look she used to have when he talked with her about his work, or said he could not talk about it with her; it was rather as if she were falling asleep at moments without knowing it.

Both Evie and Adam had become anxious because they had not heard from Sophie for some time. She had gone to the Middle East where she supposed her two friends Aisha and Amelie were, and from whom she had not heard for some time. They had undertaken to try to keep in touch with one another, because in the activities in which they hoped to be involved they had felt it important both to be separate and to feel together at the same time.

Evie opened her eyes and said 'You think she might have been pregnant?'

Adam said 'Who, Sophie?'

'No, I was thinking of that girl you were telling me about.'

'Oh. I don't know. I think she would have told me.'

'Why?'

'No, I suppose she wouldn't have wanted me in on it.'

'Why not?'

'She would have wanted to do things for herself.'

'Do you think Sophie's pregnant?'

'I don't know.'

'I used to think it was one of Sophie's friends you were talking about.'

'That I got pregnant?'

'That you behaved badly with.'

'I don't know if it was bad.'

'No, I accept that. But it wasn't one of Sophie's friends?'

'There was one of Sophie's friends. But it wasn't her. No.'

When Amelie and her British colonel had finished dinner they went out to where the darkness was lit by a building in the distance on fire, with shafts of light climbing into the sky like scaffolding. The colonel said 'We must get you out of here.' Amelie thought – But I don't want to go.

The colonel's armoured vehicle was waiting with its driver. Amelie was saying to herself – We none of us know what we are doing here: there are no masked divinities with guns telling us what to do and we having to pretend that we don't understand what they say. We are allowed an hour or two's break to have dinner, all right. But what on earth is there for us to do the rest of the time except play war games or love games, which are not so different?

Amelie said 'Do you expect to die here?' The colonel said 'No, do you?' Amelie thought – Then why do you think I should get out of here?

They drove back to the so-called compound within which the colonel's headquarters was protected. On the way there was an explosion in the distance, first the flash and the impression of pressure, and the sound coming later. The colonel said 'I'll have to leave you for a time, Jackson will look after you.' Amelie said 'I must find my crew.' The driver said 'I'm sorry, Miss, your crew have gone.' Amelie said 'They've only just arrived.' The driver said 'They were turned round at the airport.'

The colonel had jumped out of the vehicle and was running zig-zagging through the protective gates into his headquarters building. Amelie thought – All right, there may be men with masks and guns at the back of the stage, but they are not divinities.

The driver said 'Where do you want to go, Miss?'

Amelie said 'My things are in the nurse's home.'

'I'll take you there, Miss.'

'Do you know what's happening?'

'The usual I suppose.'

'Bombers? Suicide bombers? Not Iran.'

'I don't know, Miss.'

Amelie said to herself – But there are no divinities except in our heads?

At dinner the colonel had seemed to be saying that he knew his job here was doing pretty well the opposite of what was intended, but it was – what – standing up against what was otherwise the meaninglessness of life? A protest against God, if you like, if God was an old terrorist with a mask and a gun in the sky, which he wasn't, though it often enough seemed that something was. A part of ourselves, perhaps, with masks and bombs at the back of our minds. So when I asked the colonel – this was Amelie trying to make herself heard at the back of her own mind – Why shouldn't we just let people get on with killing each other and themselves if that's what they choose to do? – and indeed if that's what an orderly cycle of life-and-death seems to require – where am I, oh yes – but if we do this, aren't we just surrendering to the old terrorist in the sky and in our minds? –

– while what we should be doing –

– I mean even if a nuclear war with Iran seems to have started –

The jeep was pulling up outside the nurse's home. Another loud explosion spattered and scattered the building next door. The driver said 'We'll get a safer room for you, Miss.' She said 'No I want to stay here.' 'It's not safe, Miss.' 'I know it's not safe.' She got out of the vehicle and stood by its side so that if it began to drive off she would have a choice. She said to the driver 'I'm sorry to be a bore!' He said 'It's a pleasure, Miss.' There was shouting from the building next door; the sounds of a fire-engine or ambulance. She said 'I have to talk to the woman in charge here, she said she had something to say to me.' The driver said 'Then I'll get back.' She said 'Just wait a moment longer.' She thought – And if I get trapped under rubble, perhaps someone will finish me off here.

She said 'Is it always like this?'

The driver said 'Like what, Miss.'

'Not knowing what's happening.'

'I don't know, Miss.'

'How long have you been out here?'

'Four months.'

'Do you think you're doing any good?'

'It's a life, Miss.'

A woman in a nurse's or matron's military uniform was coming through the protective barriers in front of the nurse's home. She said 'I wondered what had happened to you.'

Amelie said 'I'm all right.'

'You don't remember me, do you?'

'I don't think so.'

'Then never mind.'

The driver said 'I'll go now, Miss.'

Amelie said 'All right, and thank you.'

The woman in uniform led the way into the building. She was older than Amelie. She said 'One summer I looked after you.'

Amelie said 'When?'

'You and your brother.'

'I haven't got a brother.'

'I must be wrong then. I can't remember. I thought I recognised you.'

'Perhaps it was my friend. She used to talk about someone who looked after her and some friends one summer.'

'Who is your friend?'

'Her name is Sophie. Her friend had a brother.'

'What did she say?'

'I don't know. There was something special about that summer.'

'Then who are you?'

'Who are you?'

There was another loud explosion close by. Bits and pieces scattered down like rain. The woman said 'I've got to get back to the wards.'

Amelie said 'Can I help?'

'Yes, if you like. There'll be injured coming in.'

'Yes I'd like.'

'One has to get on.'

'That's right.'

'I think I can work it out.'

'Good.'

'Though I don't know how it's happened.'

'No.'

'But we're lucky, we know what to do.'

'Well that's what matters, isn't it?'

When Sophie woke she found her Arab friend by the bed. He said 'You got breakfast.'

'Yes thank you. What time is it?'

'Morning.'

'I had breakfast last night!'

'You had quite a bang on the head.'

Sophie sat up. She found she had no clothes on. She held the sheet up in front of her. She thought – This is ridiculous.

Her Arab friend sat at some distance from her by the dressing table. He was dressed as usual in a white robe and elegant headdress.

She said 'Your people are very efficient.'

'They like to be.'

'How do they manage that?'

'It is the will of Allah.' He said this in a tone that might contain more than a hint of irony, or a joke.

'And how do you get them to believe that?'

'By not saying or thinking it is ridiculous.' Then – 'And by paying them.'

When he smiled he had white teeth beneath a small moustache which was like – the image came into Sophie's mind – an electric toothbrush.

She said 'I wanted to explore, but I fell asleep.'

'I would like to take you to my proper home which is some distance away. We can fly there.'

'Where?'

'On the Gulf.'

'And you would make me one of you wives?'

'If you wished. If it turned out that way.'

'You usually manage to get things your way – '

'I am rich. We have gas and oil. And yes, if it is the will of Allah.'

'All part of the same thing?'

'Of course.' This had no trace of irony.

She said 'Yes I should like to see where you live.'

She thought – I can always make a run for it at the airport. She swung herself round and put her feet on the floor.

He said 'I have brought you some clothes. They belong to one of my cousins.'

'Will she mind?'

'No.'

'I have my things in my hotel.'

'My man has gone to get them.'

'Does he know where to go?

'He seems to think so.'

Sophie thought – Well, this is all very interesting. My sandals and shoes are in the hotel, and my phone. It was because of my absurd wish to be humble that I was not properly dressed, and so had my fall. But Linn, I might never have been able to speak to you again!

She picked up a finely-spun gold-coloured garment off the bed. He did not seem to have brought any underclothes. She could not see her old shorts and T-shirt; he or the servants must have taken them? But this gold garment would reach to the ground.

He was watching her. She said 'Are you a big cheese in your country?'

He said 'A big cheese, yes.'

'And what are you trying to achieve? Except to be efficient and get your own way.'

'What more would you want?'

'But do you eliminate those who disagree with you? Keep women in subjection?'

'Is that how I have kept you?'

'No. But what are your aims: your wishes, hopes, desires?'

'To see things working smoothly.'

'The political machinery?'

'The social machinery. Every part has a function, which it accepts.'

'And that is the will of Allah?'

'Naturally.'

'But there is no chance? Hazard?'

'Hazard?'

'I mean, if things go wrong. The unexpected. Something you know you can't control.'

'And what might that be?'

'I don't know. Whatever.'

Sophie had finished dressing. There was no mirror in which to look at herself. She thought – I am now in a tent in the desert, with nothing conceivably under my control.

He said 'You are ready? You are coming?'

But he was now looking at her, she realised, as if there was something about which he was not now certain. She said 'What else would it make sense to do?'

He frowned. He said 'What do you want?'

She said 'Nothing.'

'What are you looking for?'

'What I will find.'

'You're not –'

'What?'

'Have you some information?'

'What about?'

She thought – He thinks I may be a spy: a conspirator.

He said 'All right, come along then.'

She thought – But he must know on some level that there may be a catastrophe?

The old history master was being wheeled in his chair by the one-time science mistress. They were going across what looked like a dusty plain. The history master said 'I don't see the point of this.' The science mistress said 'We're looking for the cave, or hole in the ground, in which there is said to have been found some jars, or an urn, in which there were, and may still be, some ancient scrolls, or scripts, which, when interpreted, will turn on their heads three major religions and indeed our understanding of the human race. But the only way to get in may be to smash the urn, and then the air will get in, and there will be nothing left.'

The old history master, who liked to make out he was slightly senile, said 'It looks like a film-set to me.'

The science mistress said 'It is a film-set. Unless you're going to say that everything is a film-set nowadays, what with satellite surveillance and CCTV cameras everywhere, in which case it will be even more like a film-set. Which is logical. Everyone likes a good farce.'

'That's not logical.'

'No. I hope they're paying us well.'

'Playing us well?'

'We might stop in the middle and demand more money. They'd never give in to that. We'd lose sympathy, but perhaps make a bit in the press.'

'Have a bit of a rest?'

'Have you got your hearing aids in?'

'No. Look, what's that!'

'What's what?'

'It looks like an urn.'

'It is an urn. But don't be taken in by that.'

'That's a joke? It really is an urn?'

'Yes. Or a hole in the ground. Or sometimes they call it a jar.'

'You mean it might contain whisky?'

'But if the only way to get in is to smash it – '

'That's not funny.'

The old history master man and the science mistress seemed to have lost their way, or stopped acting, or to be waiting for something to come up on an autocue. So the old master said as if improvising – 'I still think there's a difference between what's for entertainment and what's not.'

The science mistress said 'Someone must have put it there.'

'And it might have altered three major religions and the human race?'

'So they say.'

'You don't say.'

'What?'

'He didn't say.'

She said 'Didn't you say we might have a rest?'

The science mistress pushes him into the shade of a large tree that seemed to have been placed there to give an effect of surreality in the dusty plain. She sits and fans herself with her hat. The old man pushes himself a few inches to and fro restlessly in his chair.

The science mistress says 'The more you think you understand the more you know you don't, and probably never will. Is that it? But is it nothing or not?'

'It's a saying.'

'You don't say.'

'Who was that?'

'He didn't say'

'We've done that.'

'Oh so we have.'

The old history master looks round. Then he says 'Where's the producer? I want the producer! I want to get us out of here!'

'You've tried that. It doesn't work.'

'It's in the script.'

'There isn't a script.'

'You said it was in the jar.'

A voice says 'All right, open it.'

The old history master and the science mistress look round. Then they look at the ground as if embarrassed. An armoured vehicle is approaching across the dusty plain carrying soldiers holding guns. Behind this comes a larger truck carrying what looked like prisoners holding spades and pickaxes. The history master looks up and says 'Oh God, we've seen this! It was on just the other day!'

The science mistress says 'People like seeing what they feel at home with.'

'Why don't we want to see what's in that urn?'

'If we do, there'll be nothing to look forward to.'

'What will there be?'

'Dust.'

'Just dust?'

'The stuff of the universe.'

The soldiers climb out of their truck. They herd the prisoners out of their truck; then set them to work digging what it seems might be their grave.

The history master shouts 'Hold on a minute!'

The science mistress says 'Why? It's in the script.'

The history master says 'You said there wasn't any script.'

'I said it was in the jar.'

A voice says again 'All right, open it.'

The voice of the producer comes over a loudspeaker – 'Anything wrong?'

The science mistress says 'We're having a domestic quarrel.'

The history master shouts 'This is war!'

A voice shouts 'Smash the urn!'

In the ensuing silence, the voice of the producer says 'Who said that?'

The science mistress says quietly 'If you smash the urn, you'll lose the stuff that holds the universe together.'

A voice says 'I did.'

'Where are you?'

'In the urn.'

The prisoners have stopped their digging. They kneel on the ground and sift the dust carefully with their fingers. It is as if they are archaeologists who have come across something that might be of great fragility and value.

The producer says 'Can we get on?'

The history master says 'Phew, that was a close one!'

The science mistress says 'I'm still not convinced there's anything in that urn.'

'You heard it!'

'Yes I heard it.'

'And the world's still here!'

'I suppose so.'

The producer says 'Then let's get on.'

24

Linn had been instructed to travel to Iran and renew his old contacts there. He wondered if this might be a manoeuvre to have him eliminated, which would be risky to do in New York. Such speculations were not uncommon in the environment he was accustomed to; they were like fairy stories to make one feel accustomed to the otherwise inexplicable world in which one lived. They were not to be taken literally – but then was anything to be taken literally? It was as a corollary to this that he had had his fantasies about Sophie – was she connected to British Intelligence, did she have such suspicions about him; were these imaginings a symptom of the natural vulnerability of love, and did they help to divert anxiety from more personal doubts and worries. But from the beginning it had seemed to both him and Sophie that their intimacy was in some way connected to a larger and mainly unknown network – nothing to do with spies and plotting, but rather something in its essence evanescent even if overwhelming, to do with the way that the world was kept on its course. This could not be held up to much scrutiny or it would disappear like those paintings on the walls of a tomb that has been broken into.

Most of the meagre information that Linn gathered in his work remained anyway within the common speculation of anyone interested in such affairs – was or was not China supplying nuclear information to Iran, what technology was or was not Iran supplying to Iraq, was the chief effect of the British and American occupation of Iraq and Afghanistan the enormous fortunes now being made from contraband oil and heroin? And as for Linn's China – did not China just want to be seen to have as many fingers in as many pies as possible, as part of its programme to appear as an ever more dominant power?

But to talk of the countries involved in these machinations as if they were entities with the gift of conscious control – well this was of use only in the manner of belief in fairy stories.

Linn knew that Sophie was somewhere in the Middle East, but did not know just where or how to make contact with her. Her mobile phone was either out of range or out of order. He thought – We need some touch of a fairy story!

When he changed planes in Paris en route to Iran from New York, he was subjected to rigorous personal search. But this was to be expected: he was Chinese and going to Iran. And then on the night flight from Paris the man in the seat on Linn's right next to the aisle seemed to be spending a great deal of time trying and failing to take off his shoes. Of course it was known that people's feet swelled at a high altitude? But also, that there were people called shoe-bombers.

Linn drifted into speculation about what use Iranians might make of nuclear weapons that they might acquire. They would threaten to bomb Israel? But then Israel would surely nuclear-bomb Iran first. That would be how Armageddon would start, yes. Why did the Americans so resolutely back up Israel: not just to attract the Jewish vote at home, but – but as usual, oil? But the Israelis didn't have oil! The Islamists did. Oh yes, there was the fairy story that the American born-again neo-con Christians in power were expecting the end of the world and thus the second coming of Jesus, who would be likely to land on the Mount of Olives. And so the Americans wanted the Israelis rather than the Islamists to be there to welcome him. But why? Didn't the Americans know that the Israelis were historically rigorously hostile to Jesus, while Islamists regarded Jesus as some sort of true prophet? All this was an odd scenario for Armageddon. Or was it typical?

The man in the seat next to Linn on the aisle still seemed to be obsessively adjusting his shoes. Linn wondered if he should offer to give him a hand, or have a word with a steward about explosives.

He began to regret the fatalistic attitude he had shared with Sophie. He imagined now, as his plane got closer to wherever Sophie might be, that instead of travelling to put himself in the hands of his embassy people in Tehran, he might somehow get the plane to land short, and join up with Sophie somewhere on the Gulf. Hadn't she hinted that she might be pregnant? Then they might continue their fairy story about changing the world on a beach!

Perhaps if the man next to him just blew a hole in the fuselage of the plane with his shoes, it would be forced to land somewhere near where Sophie was staying, and they could have their baby there, and catch and eat fish, and be spectators of Armageddon.

He must have fallen asleep for a time because when he woke he remembered the vestige of a dream about an airport by the sea with oil-rigs in the distance, while the rest disappeared because there was some disturbance going on in the aisle. The woman opposite was talking to a steward and was gesturing towards the man with the shoes. Linn wondered – Or is it me because I am Chinese? Perhaps the aeroplane will land and I will be ejected somewhere near the sea.

The steward had turned his attention to the man with the shoes. He was an anxious-looking man with, yes, an incipient beard and a darkish skin. The steward was saying 'Excuse me sir, can I help you with your shoes?'

The man looked up at the steward as if he did not understand what he was saying.

Linn thought – But surely someone so obviously looking and behaving like a terrorist cannot be one?

The steward said 'You want to take them off?'

Linn thought – Well don't just help him!

The woman across the aisle said with a French accent 'He has been doing something with them the journey entire!'

The man turned and looked at Linn.

Linn thought – Me? I only hoped the journey might be interrupted peacefully!

A senior steward had appeared in the aisle together with a hostess. This steward said 'I'm sorry, sir, but I must insist that you let me see your shoes.' Then he fell or pounced on the man, pinioning his arms and forcing him back in his chair. The first steward and the air hostess knelt and each tried to grab a foot. Linn thought – For God's sake, you'll set them off! The man began to shout and struggle. Linn thought – Perhaps he's ticklish. The shoes seemed to fit very tightly. One or two women further down the plane started screaming. Linn said 'Shouldn't you land first and then carry out a proper – ' But they had got his shoes off. The woman across the aisle seemed to have fainted. The shoes were being turned this way and that. Linn thought – One doesn't, after all, want a proper Armageddon.

Aisha walked down the hill. She came to where Simeon had been restrained by the Israeli soldiers, who she presumed were his one-time companions in his troop of tanks. She said in English 'The officer you are holding saved my life and the life of the child. He also defended his tank, and ensured that you can recover it when you will. He also uncovered the passage by which it seems infiltrators have got into your territory, and by which perhaps some of your children have got into ours, until one of them chose of his own free will to climb back openly through the fence. So what you are doing now is, as usual, incomprehensible.'

His companions were no longer holding Simeon. One of them said 'Who are you?'

Aisha said 'I have come through the tunnel. I would like to stay in your land as your friend if you like, or if you so wish you can detain me by force.'

'Who was that child?'

'I thought you might know.'

Simeon said 'You mean, he originally came from here, and then came back without using the tunnel?'

Aisha said 'Well he did, didn't he? And wasn't it you who said that the way through which he went out, must have been a tomb?'

They stared at Aisha, until she felt she were tingling with arrows.

One of his companions said to Simeon 'And you say it was because you felt he originally came from here, that you let him back through the fence?'

Aisha said 'And when I was in the tunnel I had the impression that there were many others like him, but of course it was dark.'

Simeon said 'You came by yourself?'

'Yes.'

One of Simeon's companions said 'I think they used the tunnel to get to school.'

Another said 'What school?'

A third said 'I thought we bombed their schools.'

Aisha said 'Of course you may take all this as a fairy story if you like, but it depends how you want to live.' Then – 'One thing it can't be is the oil.' She smiled.

They stared at her. One of them said 'Oil?'

'Or do I mean nuclear capability?' Aisha seemed to try to look solemn.

Simeon was saying to Aisha 'Where will you stay?'

Aisha was saying 'I thought you might help me.'

Simeon said 'You think you knew that child?'

'No more than you.'

'I asked you if you wanted a child.'

'If there is an environment left for it.'

One of Simeon's companions said 'What did you mean about our nuclear capability?'

Aisha said 'Well it isn't a child, is it?'

Two or three of the villagers who had been grouped on the football field began to kick a ball about. The soldiers around Simeon watched them.

The Old Man said to Lilith 'You and I may not have to spend so much time keeping an eye on the incredibly boring sights over this precipice soon.'

Lilith said 'You mean, there'll either be something worth seeing, or nothing?'

The British commander came into the room in the nurse's home where Amelie was sitting on a bed with her arms drooped between her knees. He said 'I thought you'd gone.'

She said 'No, I was helping in the hospital.'

'Your crew were turned back. I thought I'd missed you.'

'I don't want my crew. They were getting rather fed up with me.'

'You'd better go. There's more information coming through.'

'About what?'

'The bombing.'

'Go where?'

'Anywhere.'

'You think one can get away from it?'

The colonel came and sat on the end of her bed. He said 'No.'

She said 'So everything's happening all at once. Bombs, nuclear proliferation, global warming, and that strange beast slouching towards Bethlehem to be reborn.'

'It's not reborn, it's born.'

'That makes a difference?'

'Yes. Nothing's really been tried yet.'

Amelie lay back on the bed. She put her hands behind her head. She said 'The head nurse here thinks she remembers me. Which is both impossible and possible. When I was in Iran there was a girl who was killed or perhaps not killed who I thought I knew at school. Ditto.'

The colonel said 'Yes?'

Amelie said 'This isn't a seduction scene. Except perhaps to try to get God interested.' She laughed, and raised her arms. She said 'Oh God come down!'

The colonel said 'You frighten me.'

Amelie said 'But he did, didn't he?'

'And look what we do to him.'

'So we simply stop.'

'Stop what?'

She sat up in bed and looked at him. She said 'I'm an Israeli. I'm a Jew. There's nothing I can do.'

'Why not?'

'We do what we're told.'

'What are you told?'

'Nothing.'

'Nothing?'

'It stopped years ago.'

'What?'

'We make it ourselves.'

'What?'

'Whatever. I'm a Christian I'm a Muslim.'

'You're saying there's no God.'

'I'm saying of course there's a God! How else could we make anything!'

The colonel put his hand on her leg. He said 'I thought you wanted children.'

'Did I say that?'

'Maybe not.'

'Was that why you were frightened?'

'Maybe.'

She sat up in the bed again. She said 'Look, whatever's happening at this moment, we've got to keep watching and listening.'

'Well I'm grateful.'

'Thank you.'

'Will you go on filming?'

'I suppose so. Will you go on being a soldier?'

'I suppose so.'

'Well I don't see why we shouldn't try it and see what happens.'
She held out her arms to him.

Adam looked at what he had written on his computer –

> In the early years of the twenty-first century it began to be
> felt that there was a real possibility of the world, or at least
> the human species, coming to an end; both because humans
> now seemed to have the technical means to achieve this,
> and because there had evolved political and emotional pre-
> dicaments that seemed insoluble except through violent
> confrontation – this apparently being an intrinsic part of
> nature's style of evolution. Oh God this is so boring. The

coming-into-being and then the expansion of the State of
Israel in what Arabs regarded as their homeland – together
with historical and metaphysical conditions which seemed
to make it impossible for Arabs and Jews to compromise –
for God's sake don't go into these – had come to a pass from
which there seemed to be no outcome because there was
neither authority nor common sense to appeal to. Or in
other words, because that's the sort of shit they liked. The
Israelis claimed that the land had been given to them
through Abraham and Moses several thousand years ago –
haven't I already said this several thousand times? – although most of their politicians who now go to such
lengths to enforce this are no longer loyal to historical Judaism except for political ends. God help them. There were
certain devout Jews however who believed that political
ends were a betrayal of Judaism anyway – yes I know I've
said this, I know I should be getting on to what really
matters, which is – oh yes – the realisation that freedom,
autonomy, cannot be established by political means, nor
does it naturally come about if left to itself; it can only be
nurtured, flourish, if it is allied to a sense of God. And God
has done his best with this, God knows – how does the
old song go – There was a man who tried and tried, but his
wife was never satisfied – Oh for God's sake! I will find
myself in a mass grave for this sort of thing! – And so he
built a great machine, and the whole fucking issue was
driven by steam – And so on. A song both obscene and
blasphemous. The machine being what – church, churches,
synagogues, mosques: all right, any hijacking of religion
into systems of power. But this drunken bar-room song

might be taken not only to be about God's efforts to care for humans while leaving them free, but also, heaven help us, about humans' rediscovery of their true need for God through darkness and disaster. Though most of the rest of the song is unprintable even by me. Except, of course, for the lovely unexpected end about the burgeoning of violets. How does it go – But this is a story of the bitter bit, there was no means of stopping it – And then. But all right, stop it! Stop it!

Adam pushed himself back so violently in his chair that the wheels on which it rested snagged, and he found himself falling over backwards with his arms flailing. He thought – My God, I am like that man on his bike going over the cliff! But I will never make it beyond the rocks, is that what I am saying? I will crash and that will be the end of me, and good riddance, and of such gross impropriety. His head hit the edge of a metal filing cabinet somewhere behind him. He thought – All right, I'm sorry, God, no I'm not sorry, what the hell! He was lying on his back staring at the ceiling with pain in his head beginning to suffuse him. He thought – But doesn't resurrection come after pain and filth? Or – Oh all right, let me die then.

He tried to push himself up into a sitting position or to roll over on his side, but there was now also a pain in his back when he tried to move. So he thought – All right, old Daddy, old kamerad, I'm kaput! Then he waved his arms and legs in the air and said – Woo hoo, I'm a baby! Then – But how was it that that song came to end not with shit but with sweet violets – the Holy Spirit?

He wondered if he did a backward somersault thus keeping his spine untwisted this would avoid the pain in his back. Or would he become permanently paralysed with his groin pressed into his face

– a not uncommon human predicament. That would teach him! Or perhaps he should stay quiet for a time until Evie came to rescue him.

In the meantime what should he think about: Sophie? Aisha? Amelie? Perhaps that girl he had called Suzie?

Politics led to violence. That was nature. You tried to ignore it or mock it, and you landed up under a filing cabinet. Was this God's sense of humour?

What was all the stuff about babies that kept coming in? Chance enters as a component of the genetic code? As babies? Was this science?

What about the girl who had made such a show on the steps? Was she Suzie?

And all shall be well and all manner of things shall be well. This was God.

Evie came into the room. At first she could not see him, because he was on the floor behind the desk. Then she said 'What on earth are you doing? I heard a crash.'

He said 'I was being irreverent. I fell into a tomb.'

'What happened?'

'I'd just seen an answer to all the stuff at the centre of the universe. Which was both witty and obscene. Then I was struck by a thunderbolt.

'You're being boring again.'

'Born again. Ha ha. Yes. One of my terrible jokes. I've got some of them in too.'

He found that he was struggling to his feet without too much difficulty. He wondered if he should press 'Save' for the stuff he'd written on his computer, or should he leave that, of all things, to chance.

Evie said 'Will you come downstairs. There's someone on television talking about Iran.'

'Have they done their bomb yet?'

'I don't know.'

He began to go with Evie to the door. Then he lurched back and pressed the requisite keys on the computer. Then he followed Evie down the stairs. He said 'You know the theory that it's only when politically incorrect jokes have become acceptable that racial and religious distinctions will be over – '

Evie said 'I want to make a confession.'

' – well I think this applies to distinctions between God and humans.'

'Are you listening?'

'Yes.' He thought – A confession before the bomb goes off?

She said 'I did something stupid the other day.'

'Oh, I have wondered.'

'Don't you want to know what it was?'

'Yes. Or not unless you want to tell me.'

'What was the name of that *au pair* you had a go with?'

'I don't know. Suzie. I mean I call her Suzie. Why?'

In the sitting room there was a man in the uniform of a colonel talking on television. He was saying that as far as he was concerned whatever it was was irrelevant. And he should know, because he lived on the job, and most things were irrelevant.

'She sent a message saying she'd met someone who knew Sophie, and she hoped that Sophie was all right.'

'Who did?'

'Your *au pair*. But it sounded as if she was called something quite different.'

'Yes her name was very complicated. But why didn't you tell me?'

'I thought she must be trying to get in touch with you.'

'Well wouldn't it be nice if she was?'

'Well I've said I'm sorry. She did sound very nice.'

Adam sat down. He felt his head where he had banged it. It seemed to be in one piece.

He said 'She thought Sophie might not be all right? Why? Where is Sophie?'

'That last letter you had was from Aleppo.'

'Where's Aleppo? I mean I know where Aleppo is. Where is it in relation to Iran? Yes I know that. My head's still a bit wobbly, sorry.' Then – 'I can't remember her real name.'

'Whose?'

'Suzie's.'

'You've put her in your book?'

'Oh I don't know who or what is what I've put in my book!'

The colonel on television was saying he had absolutely nothing more to say on television. There was a girl in the background that Adam thought for a moment he recognised; but it might be that one could recognise anything. Then the picture switched back to the studio.

Adam thought – Perhaps I am bonkers. Or perhaps the next mutation in the brain will be an awareness of connections that one is not conscious of, but of which one is conscious of not being conscious. Commonly called bonkers.

He said 'How can we find out?'

'What?'

'About Sophie. Where she is now. If she's all right.'

'The last thing she said to me on her mobile was that she'd like to have triplets.'

'Triplets!'

'I think it was a joke.'

Adam was thinking – But did what-was-her-name leave an address?

On the screen there was a picture of a crowded hospital ward with bodies doubling up on beds and on the floor. Doctors and nurses in masks were attending to them.

Evie said 'You're not angry?'

'Why should I be angry?'

'About my not telling you. She said she might get in touch with us when she's next in England.'

'That's very good of you. I mean good of her. Where is she now?'

'Iran I think. Or Iraq. She says you saved her life.'

Adam thought – Oh well, that does make a big difference, yes.

Then – And I suppose I do not really need to know what happened to you, Evie, on your night out.

On television the presenter was talking about a report that peace talks between Israelis and Palestinians were about to resume; though this did not necessarily mean anything because there had been so many such stories before.

The Old Man is saying to Lilith – Well, they do seem to be getting to know a bit more about what they don't know.

Lilith says – Yes, and that it can seem quite funny.

– What was the end of the song that fellow was singing?

– It's not printable.

– Well that's a mercy. Then they won't be able to misinterpret it.

– Don't bank on that.

– But they do seem to be beginning to be able to take over?

– Yes. And the happy end comes as quite a shock.

The Old Man thinks – You mean, the Holy Spirit?

Sophie came down the steps from her Arab friend's private plane onto the tarmac which was like the hot plate of a cooker. Surrounding the runway and the airport buildings were huge stretches of sand as if a precaution against fire. Beyond these there was what might once have been the sanctuary of the sea, but this now sprouted oil-rig platforms like bones breaking through skin and thus open to infection. Sophie thought – What once was life-blood, now is disease.

A car was waiting on the tarmac. It seemed there would be no formality about identity papers for Sophie. Her Arab friend, for whom she still knew no name, was engaged in conversation with the driver of the car who had got out and was standing as if to attention on the tarmac.

Sophie thought – How relevant that such a desert should have become a fount of worldly riches!

– But did riches ever give power?

On the coast was the bulk of a power station or a processing plant, perhaps one to make drinking water out of the sea? She thought – Humans organise what they can of resources; but this still is not power.

The driver was holding open a door of the car. She climbed in. Her Arab friend climbed in after her. He said 'There has been some alarm on the airwaves.'

She said 'Such as – '

'Bombs and rumours of bombs.'

The driver was manipulating a telephone in the front compartment of the large car. The sun made the inside of the car very hot. Sophie thought – But if one sweats, perhaps one doesn't have to pee.

The driver and her Arab friend were having a conversation in a language that Sophie did not understand. The car was still not moving.

Sophie thought – Perhaps bombs and rumours of bombs means we will have to stay on at the airport. I will not ask what is happening. I will believe I am learning something about the relationship between God and Humans.

The driver was trying to hand the telephone to her Arab friend. He was brushing it away. He said to Sophie 'I am sorry for the delay. We may have to get back on to the plane.'

Sophie said 'Won't we have to refuel?'

He friend looked slightly put out by this. He said 'That is a good point.'

Then he said something further in their language to the driver, who got out and walked to the plane, and stood and called up to the window of the cockpit.

On their flight there had been a pilot and a co-pilot and a stewardess. Sophie thought – Perhaps they are all taking the chance to have sex.

She said 'What will you do when the oil runs out? Or will you be developing nuclear technology?'

The driver was turning back towards the car and raising his forearms in a gesture of impotence.

Sophie's friend said 'What?'

Sophie said 'I mean, the idea that everything works according to the will of Allah is all right with something like oil, because that's what you can control, and to call it the will of Allah I suppose increases your authority. But as things get more complex they depend more on chance, and that you can't control. So then the will of Allah becomes what you don't know, not what you do.'

Her Arab friend muttered something angrily, then flung the door of the car open and lunged out. Then he turned back and put his face on a level with the open window and said 'You can do what you like. I am not responsible.' Then he set off across the tarmac towards the plane.

Sophie thought – Yes, and your life is mostly very boring.

There was the noise of a plane in the air approaching, getting louder, perhaps coming in to land; but the runway seemed to be blocked by her Arab friend's plane. Or of course there was a second runway; or was the new plane one of the kind that crashed into an airport building. Then she saw her Arab friend and his driver throw themselves face down on the tarmac as the plane came in very low overhead with a roar and a rush of wind; a huge plane, some jumbo jet, perhaps having to make an emergency landing. So was that something that one could or couldn't control?

Had she offended her Arab friend? Had she insulted the prophet Mohammed? Had she been right about atomic energy? Figures had begun to run out of the airport building; then turned and ran back. The huge plane had hit the ground some way ahead of where Sophie sat in the car; it half bounced and skidded, then slewed round with the tip of one wing on the sand. Bits of structure and sparks broke off and whizzed along the ground like insects. Perhaps the under-carriage had not worked? But in such a situation it was ridiculous to sit in a car. She got out and closed the door behind her. She put a hand up to shield her eyes.

Her Arab friend had returned to the car. He said 'Get back in.'
She said 'No.'
'There may be an explosion.'
'Then people will need help.'

There were sounds of police or ambulance sirens from the direction of the airport building. Sophie began to walk across the tarmac to where the plane was lying twisted on the sand. She thought – It was time I said a few No's to my Arab friend.

There were people beginning to emerge from the plane by emergency steps and chutes. Ambulances and a police car and a fire-engine were arriving. Sophie still had some way to go. The Arab man did not seem to be coming after her.

She thought – But if I am pregnant I may need someone to look after me.

Would Lilith be saying – Will this do?

The Old Man would be saying – Yes I think so.

Sophie saw Linn coming down the emergency steps from the plane. She thought – Now no big deal, please. Why should not this occurrence be just as natural as one brick on top of another? She said 'Hello! What a time you must have been having!' Linn said 'Yes, and you too!' He was looking over her shoulder at the Arab man who was now hurrying up after her. Sophie, between the two of them, half turned and said 'This is my friend Linn; and this is another friend, I'm afraid I don't know your name. He's been very good to me, he got me here most efficiently.' She laughed. She thought – Well, we all need all the help we can get. Linn said 'There was a man on our plane who said he knew that our undercarriage wasn't working because he could feel vibrations in his feet. No one believed him.' Linn laughed. From a long way off the driver of the car was waving to them. Sophie's Arab friend held out his hand to Linn, who took it. He said 'Can I give you a lift? Do you know where you're going?' Then – 'Oh no, you wouldn't, would you!' Then – 'Nor do I at the moment.' They all found themselves laughing.

SELECTED DALKEY ARCHIVE PAPERBACKS

Petros Abatzoglou, *What Does Mrs. Freeman Want?*
Michal Ajvaz, *The Other City.*
Pierre Albert-Birot, *Grabinoulor.*
Yuz Aleshkovsky, *Kangaroo.*
Felipe Alfau, *Chromos.*
　Locos.
Ivan Ângelo, *The Celebration.*
　The Tower of Glass.
David Antin, *Talking.*
António Lobo Antunes, *Knowledge of Hell.*
Alain Arias-Misson, *Theatre of Incest.*
John Ashbery and James Schuyler, *A Nest of Ninnies.*
Djuna Barnes, *Ladies Almanack.*
　Ryder.
John Barth, *LETTERS.*
　Sabbatical.
Donald Barthelme, *The King.*
　Paradise.
Svetislav Basara, *Chinese Letter.*
Mark Binelli, *Sacco and Vanzetti Must Die!*
Andrei Bitov, *Pushkin House.*
Louis Paul Boon, *Chapel Road.*
　Summer in Termuren.
Roger Boylan, *Killoyle.*
Ignácio de Loyola Brandão, *Anonymous Celebrity.*
　Teeth under the Sun.
　Zero.
Bonnie Bremser, *Troia: Mexican Memoirs.*
Christine Brooke-Rose, *Amalgamemnon.*
Brigid Brophy, *In Transit.*
Meredith Brosnan, *Mr. Dynamite.*
Gerald L. Bruns,
　Modern Poetry and the Idea of Language.
Evgeny Bunimovich and J. Kates, eds.,
　Contemporary Russian Poetry: An Anthology.
Gabrielle Burton, *Heartbreak Hotel.*
Michel Butor, *Degrees.*
　Mobile.
　Portrait of the Artist as a Young Ape.
G. Cabrera Infante, *Infante's Inferno.*
　Three Trapped Tigers.
Julieta Campos, *The Fear of Losing Eurydice.*
Anne Carson, *Eros the Bittersweet.*
Camilo José Cela, *Christ versus Arizona.*
　The Family of Pascual Duarte.
　The Hive.
Louis-Ferdinand Céline, *Castle to Castle.*
　Conversations with Professor Y.
　London Bridge.
　Normance.
　North.
　Rigadoon.
Hugo Charteris, *The Tide Is Right.*
Jerome Charyn, *The Tar Baby.*
Marc Cholodenko, *Mordechai Schamz.*
Emily Holmes Coleman, *The Shutter of Snow.*
Robert Coover, *A Night at the Movies.*
Stanley Crawford, *Log of the S.S. The Mrs Unguentine.*
　Some Instructions to My Wife.
Robert Creeley, *Collected Prose.*
René Crevel, *Putting My Foot in It.*
Ralph Cusack, *Cadenza.*
Susan Daitch, *L.C.*
　Storytown.
Nicholas Delbanco, *The Count of Concord.*
Nigel Dennis, *Cards of Identity.*
Peter Dimock,
　A Short Rhetoric for Leaving the Family.
Ariel Dorfman, *Konfidenz.*
Coleman Dowell, *The Houses of Children.*
　Island People.
　Too Much Flesh and Jabez.
Arkadii Dragomoshchenko, *Dust.*
Rikki Ducornet, *The Complete Butcher's Tales.*
　The Fountains of Neptune.
　The Jade Cabinet.
　The One Marvelous Thing.
　Phosphor in Dreamland.
　The Stain.
　The Word "Desire."
William Eastlake, *The Bamboo Bed.*
　Castle Keep.
　Lyric of the Circle Heart.
Jean Echenoz, *Chopin's Move.*
Stanley Elkin, *A Bad Man.*
　Boswell: A Modern Comedy.
　Criers and Kibitzers, Kibitzers and Criers.
　The Dick Gibson Show.
　The Franchiser.
　George Mills.
　The Living End.
　The MacGuffin.
　The Magic Kingdom.
　Mrs. Ted Bliss.
　The Rabbi of Lud.
　Van Gogh's Room at Arles.
Annie Ernaux, *Cleaned Out.*
Lauren Fairbanks, *Muzzle Thyself.*
　Sister Carrie.

Juan Filloy, *Op Oloop.*
Leslie A. Fiedler, *Love and Death in the American Novel.*
Gustave Flaubert, *Bouvard and Pécuchet.*
Kass Fleisher, *Talking out of School.*
Ford Madox Ford, *The March of Literature.*
Jon Fosse, *Melancholy.*
Max Frisch, *I'm Not Stiller.*
　Man in the Holocene.
Carlos Fuentes, *Christopher Unborn.*
　Distant Relations.
　Terra Nostra.
　Where the Air Is Clear.
Janice Galloway, *Foreign Parts.*
　The Trick Is to Keep Breathing.
William H. Gass, *Cartesian Sonata and Other Novellas.*
　Finding a Form.
　A Temple of Texts.
　The Tunnel.
　Willie Masters' Lonesome Wife.
Gérard Gavarry, *Hoplla! 1 2 3.*
Etienne Gilson, *The Arts of the Beautiful.*
　Forms and Substances in the Arts.
C. S. Giscombe, *Giscome Road.*
　Here.
　Prairie Style.
Douglas Glover, *Bad News of the Heart.*
　The Enamoured Knight.
Witold Gombrowicz, *A Kind of Testament.*
Karen Elizabeth Gordon, *The Red Shoes.*
Georgi Gospodinov, *Natural Novel.*
Juan Goytisolo, *Count Julian.*
　Juan the Landless.
　Makbara.
　Marks of Identity.
Patrick Grainville, *The Cave of Heaven.*
Henry Green, *Back.*
　Blindness.
　Concluding.
　Doting.
　Nothing.
Jiří Gruša, *The Questionnaire.*
Gabriel Gudding, *Rhode Island Notebook.*
John Hawkes, *Whistlejacket.*
Aidan Higgins, *A Bestiary.*
　Bornholm Night-Ferry.
　Flotsam and Jetsam.
　Langrishe, Go Down.
　Scenes from a Receding Past.
　Windy Arbours.
Aldous Huxley, *Antic Hay.*
　Crome Yellow.
　Point Counter Point.
　Those Barren Leaves.
　Time Must Have a Stop.
Mikhail Iossel and Jeff Parker, eds., *Amerika: Contemporary Russians View the United States.*
Gert Jonke, *Geometric Regional Novel.*
　Homage to Czerny.
Jacques Jouet, *Mountain R.*
　Savage.
Hugh Kenner, *The Counterfeiters.*
　Flaubert, Joyce and Beckett: The Stoic Comedians.
　Joyce's Voices.
Danilo Kiš, *Garden, Ashes.*
　A Tomb for Boris Davidovich.
Anita Konkka, *A Fool's Paradise.*
George Konrád, *The City Builder.*
Tadeusz Konwicki, *A Minor Apocalypse.*
　The Polish Complex.
Menis Koumandareas, *Koula.*
Elaine Kraf, *The Princess of 72nd Street.*
Jim Krusoe, *Iceland.*
Ewa Kuryluk, *Century 21.*
Eric Laurrent, *Do Not Touch.*
Violette Leduc, *La Bâtarde.*
Deborah Levy, *Billy and Girl.*
　Pillow Talk in Europe and Other Places.
José Lezama Lima, *Paradiso.*
Rosa Liksom, *Dark Paradise.*
Osman Lins, *Avalovara.*
　The Queen of the Prisons of Greece.
Alf Mac Lochlainn, *The Corpus in the Library.*
　Out of Focus.
Ron Loewinsohn, *Magnetic Field(s).*
Brian Lynch, *The Winner of Sorrow.*
D. Keith Mano, *Take Five.*
Micheline Aharonian Marcom, *The Mirror in the Well.*
Ben Marcus, *The Age of Wire and String.*
Wallace Markfield, *Teitlebaum's Window.*
　To an Early Grave.
David Markson, *Reader's Block.*
　Springer's Progress.
　Wittgenstein's Mistress.
Carole Maso, *AVA.*
Ladislav Matejka and Krystyna Pomorska, eds., *Readings in Russian Poetics: Formalist and Structuralist Views.*

FOR A FULL LIST OF PUBLICATIONS, VISIT:
www.dalkeyarchive.com

SELECTED DALKEY ARCHIVE PAPERBACKS

HARRY MATHEWS,
The Case of the Persevering Maltese: Collected Essays.
Cigarettes.
The Conversions.
The Human Country: New and Collected Stories.
The Journalist.
My Life in CIA.
Singular Pleasures.
The Sinking of the Odradek Stadium.
Tlooth.
20 Lines a Day.
ROBERT L. MCLAUGHLIN, ED.,
*Innovations: An Anthology of Modern &
Contemporary Fiction.*
HERMAN MELVILLE, *The Confidence-Man.*
AMANDA MICHALOPOULOU, *I'd Like.*
STEVEN MILLHAUSER, *The Barnum Museum.*
In the Penny Arcade.
RALPH J. MILLS, JR., *Essays on Poetry.*
OLIVE MOORE, *Spleen.*
NICHOLAS MOSLEY, *Accident.*
Assassins.
Catastrophe Practice.
Children of Darkness and Light.
Experience and Religion.
God's Hazard.
The Hesperides Tree.
Hopeful Monsters.
Imago Bird.
Impossible Object.
Inventing God.
Judith.
Look at the Dark.
Natalie Natalia.
Paradoxes of Peace.
Serpent.
Time at War.
The Uses of Slime Mould: Essays of Four Decades.
WARREN MOTTE,
Fables of the Novel: French Fiction since 1990.
Fiction Now: The French Novel in the 21st Century.
Oulipo: A Primer of Potential Literature.
YVES NAVARRE, *Our Share of Time.*
Sweet Tooth.
DOROTHY NELSON, *In Night's City.*
Tar and Feathers.
WILFRIDO D. NOLLEDO, *But for the Lovers.*
FLANN O'BRIEN, *At Swim-Two-Birds.*
At War.
The Best of Myles.
The Dalkey Archive.
Further Cuttings.
The Hard Life.
The Poor Mouth.
The Third Policeman.
CLAUDE OLLIER, *The Mise-en-Scène.*
PATRIK OUŘEDNÍK, *Europeana.*
FERNANDO DEL PASO, *News from the Empire.*
Palinuro of Mexico.
ROBERT PINGET, *The Inquisitory.*
Mahu or The Material.
Trio.
MANUEL PUIG, *Betrayed by Rita Hayworth.*
RAYMOND QUENEAU, *The Last Days.*
Odile.
Pierrot Mon Ami.
Saint Glinglin.
ANN QUIN, *Berg.*
Passages.
Three.
Tripticks.
ISHMAEL REED, *The Free-Lance Pallbearers.*
The Last Days of Louisiana Red.
Reckless Eyeballing.
The Terrible Threes.
The Terrible Twos.
Yellow Back Radio Broke-Down.
JEAN RICARDOU, *Place Names.*
RAINER MARIA RILKE,
The Notebooks of Malte Laurids Brigge.
JULIÁN RÍOS, *Larva: A Midsummer Night's Babel.*
Poundemonium.
AUGUSTO ROA BASTOS, *I the Supreme.*
OLIVIER ROLIN, *Hotel Crystal.*
JACQUES ROUBAUD, *The Form of a City Changes Faster,
Alas, Than the Human Heart.*
The Great Fire of London.
Hortense in Exile.
Hortense Is Abducted.
The Loop.
The Plurality of Worlds of Lewis.
The Princess Hoppy.
Some Thing Black.
LEON S. ROUDIEZ, *French Fiction Revisited.*

VEDRANA RUDAN, *Night.*
LYDIE SALVAYRE, *The Company of Ghosts.*
Everyday Life.
The Lecture.
The Power of Flies.
LUIS RAFAEL SÁNCHEZ, *Macho Camacho's Beat.*
SEVERO SARDUY, *Cobra & Maitreya.*
NATHALIE SARRAUTE, *Do You Hear Them?*
Martereau.
The Planetarium.
ARNO SCHMIDT, *Collected Stories.*
Nobodaddy's Children.
CHRISTINE SCHUTT, *Nightwork.*
GAIL SCOTT, *My Paris.*
DAMION SEARLS, *What We Were Doing and Where We
Were Going.*
JUNE AKERS SEESE,
Is This What Other Women Feel Too?
What Waiting Really Means.
BERNARD SHARE, *Inish.*
Transit.
AURELIE SHEEHAN, *Jack Kerouac Is Pregnant.*
VIKTOR SHKLOVSKY, *Knight's Move.*
A Sentimental Journey: Memoirs 1917–1922.
Energy of Delusion: A Book on Plot.
Literature and Cinematography.
Theory of Prose.
Third Factory.
Zoo, or Letters Not about Love.
JOSEF ŠKVORECKÝ,
The Engineer of Human Souls.
CLAUDE SIMON, *The Invitation.*
GILBERT SORRENTINO, *Aberration of Starlight.*
Blue Pastoral.
Crystal Vision.
Imaginative Qualities of Actual Things.
Mulligan Stew.
Pack of Lies.
Red the Fiend.
The Sky Changes.
Something Said.
Splendide-Hôtel.
Steelwork.
Under the Shadow.
W. M. SPACKMAN, *The Complete Fiction.*
GERTRUDE STEIN, *Lucy Church Amiably.*
The Making of Americans.
A Novel of Thank You.
PIOTR SZEWC, *Annihilation.*
STEFAN THEMERSON, *Hobson's Island.*
The Mystery of the Sardine.
Tom Harris.
JEAN-PHILIPPE TOUSSAINT, *The Bathroom.*
Camera.
Monsieur.
Television.
DUMITRU TSEPENEAG, *Pigeon Post.*
The Necessary Marriage.
Vain Art of the Fugue.
ESTHER TUSQUETS, *Stranded.*
DUBRAVKA UGRESIC, *Lend Me Your Character.*
Thank You for Not Reading.
MATI UNT, *Brecht at Night*
Diary of a Blood Donor.
Things in the Night.
ÁLVARO URIBE AND OLIVIA SEARS, EDS.,
The Best of Contemporary Mexican Fiction.
ELOY URROZ, *The Obstacles.*
LUISA VALENZUELA, *He Who Searches.*
PAUL VERHAEGHEN, *Omega Minor.*
MARJA-LIISA VARTIO, *The Parson's Widow.*
BORIS VIAN, *Heartsnatcher.*
AUSTRYN WAINHOUSE, *Hedyphagetica.*
PAUL WEST, *Words for a Deaf Daughter & Gala.*
CURTIS WHITE, *America's Magic Mountain.*
The Idea of Home.
Memories of My Father Watching TV.
*Monstrous Possibility: An Invitation to
Literary Politics.*
Requiem.
DIANE WILLIAMS, *Excitability: Selected Stories.*
Romancer Erector.
DOUGLAS WOOLF, *Wall to Wall.*
Ya! & John-Juan.
JAY WRIGHT, *Polynomials and Pollen.*
The Presentable Art of Reading Absence.
PHILIP WYLIE, *Generation of Vipers.*
MARGUERITE YOUNG, *Angel in the Forest.*
Miss MacIntosh, My Darling.
REYOUNG, *Unbabbling.*
ZORAN ŽIVKOVIĆ, *Hidden Camera.*
LOUIS ZUKOFSKY, *Collected Fiction.*
SCOTT ZWIREN, *God Head.*

FOR A FULL LIST OF PUBLICATIONS, VISIT:
www.dalkeyarchive.com